For Reference

Not to be taken from this room

Memorable Days in Music

compiled by

Marion Elizabeth Cullen

The Scarecrow Press, Inc.

Metuchen, N.J.   1970

71-8930

In
Grateful Memory
of
my beloved teacher
Ethel Newcomb
and all musical descendants of
the Vienna Master
Theodor Leschetizky

Preparatory Note

It has been my purpose not only to make this
volume a helpful Year Book, but also a compilation
of popular quotations regarding music, which may
render it useful for reference.

M. E. C.

Table of Contents

JANUARY

Music is a beautiful and glorious
gift of God.--Praetorius

January First

The Church music of Gabrieli, with the answering
choirs and its accompanying strings and trombones,
is to music what an Assumption of Titian is to
painting.--Ambros

Giovanni Gabrieli became first organist at St. Mark's Cathedral on January 1, 1585.

World premiere of Brahms' Violin Concerto in D Major was presented in Leipzig on January 1, 1879.

Gustav Mahler gave his Metropolitan debut January 1, 1908, with an impressive performance of Wagner's "Tristan und Isolde."

Johann Christian Bach died January 1, 1782.

January Second

Music is the inarticulate speech of the heart, which
cannot be compressed into words, because it is in-
finite.--Wagner

World premiere of Wagner's "The Flying Dutchman" was given in Dresden on January 2, 1843, with the composer conducting. Wilhelmine Schroder-Devrient created the role of Senta.

Michael Tippett was born January 2, 1905.

Tito Schipa was born January 2, 1889.

American debut of Glen Gould took place January 2, 1955, in Washington, D. C.

7

Toscanini conducted the Metropolitan premiere of Montemezzi's "L'Amore dei tre re" on January 2, 1914.

Karl Goldmark died January 2, 1915.

Mischa Levitzki died January 2, 1941.

Mily Balakirev was born January 2, 1837.

Arthur Rodzinski was born January 2, 1894.

Julian Gayarre died January 2, 1890.

January Third

> Let not a day pass, if possible, without having heard some fine music, read a noble poem, or seen a beautiful picture. --Goethe

Henriette Sontag was born January 3, 1806.

American premiere of Brahms' First Symphony was presented January 3, 1878, in Boston.

Mary Garden introduced "Louise" to America at the Manhattan Opera House on January 3, 1908.

Mary Garden died January 3, 1967.

Lily Pons made her sensational Metropolitan debut January 3, 1931, in "Lucia di Lammermoor."

Boris Blacher was born January 3, 1903.

Operatic debut of Giuseppini Grassini took place on January 3, 1789.

American debut of Wilhelm Furtwaengler took place in Carnegie Hall when he led the New York Philharmonic Orchestra on January 3, 1925.

Giuseppina Grassini died January 3, 1850.

January Fourth
                              Music dwells
          Lingering, and wandering on as loth to die,
          Like thoughts whose very sweetness yieldeth proof
          That they were born for immortality. --Wordsworth

Metropolitan premiere of "Die Meistersinger von Nürnberg"
was presented January 4, 1886.

World premiere of "Don Pasquale" was given at the Theatre-
Italien in Paris on January 4, 1843.

Jussi Bjorling gave his first New York concert January 4, 1938.

American premiere of Saint-Saens' opera "Samson et Dalila"
was given in New Orleans on January 4, 1893.

Metropolitan premiere of "Das Rheingold" took place January
4, 1889 with Max Alvary and Emil Fischer heading the cast.
Anton Seidl conducted.

Grace Bumbry was born January 4, 1937.

Giovanni Pergolesi was born January 4, 1710.

Gaetano Merola was born January 4, 1881.

January Fifth

          I verily think, and am not ashamed to say,
          that, next to divinity, no art is comparable
          to music. --Martin Luther

Wilhelm Backhaus made his American debut on January 5,
1912, playing the Beethoven Emperor Concerto with the New
York Symphony Orchestra, directed by Walter Damrosch.

American debut of Philippe Entremont took place on January
5, 1953, in New York City.

Wieland Wagner, director of the Bayreuth Festival and grand-
son of Richard Wagner, was born January 5, 1917.

Erica Morini was born January 5, 1910.

Nicholas Medtner was born January 5, 1880.

Frederick Shepherd Converse was born January 5, 1871.

January Sixth

> Inspiration is after all the noblest attribute in an
> artist. --Hauptmann

Alexander Scriabin was born January 6, 1872.

Emma Calvé died January 6, 1942.

Mary Costa made her bow at the Metropolitan Opera as
Violetta in "La Traviata" on January 6, 1964.

Vladimar de Pachman died January 6, 1933.

Elliot Carter's Piano Concerto was given its first performance
at the Boston Symphony Concerts on January 6, 1967.

Xaver Scharwenka was born January 6, 1850.

Max Bruch was born January 6, 1838.

January Seventh

> When Thalberg played a melody it stood out in bold
> dynamic relief; not because he pounded, but because
> he kept the accompaniment duly subdued--Christiani

Sigismund Thalberg was born January 7, 1812.

World premiere of Liszt's Second Piano Concerto was given
at the Grand Ducal Theatre in Weimar on January 7, 1857,
with the composer conducting.   Hans von Bronsart was
soloist.

Francis Poulenc was born January 7, 1899.

Ignaz Friedman made his American debut January 7, 1921,
in New York City.

Marion Anderson made her debut in opera at the Metropolitan
Opera as Ulrica in "Un Ballo in Maschera" on January 7,
1955.

Adamo Didur died January 7, 1946.

John Brownlee was born January 7, 1900.

Clara Haskil was born January 7, 1895.

World premiere of "The Emperor Jones" was presented January 7, 1933, at the Metropolitan Opera in New York.
Lawrence Tibbett had the title role.

Carl Schuricht died January 7, 1967.

January Eighth

> O Music
> In your depths we deposit our hearts and souls
> Thou hast taught us to see with our ears
> And hear with our hearts. --Kahlil Gibran

New York debut of Artur Rubinstein took place January 8, 1906.

Handel's first opera "Almeria" was produced on January 8, 1705.

Joan Sutherland sang the role of Violetta in "La Traviata" at Covent Garden on January 8, 1960.

Hans von Bulow was born January 8, 1830.

Arcangelo Corelli died January 8, 1713.

Jaromir Weinberger was born January 8, 1896.

January Ninth

> In music you will soon find out what personal benefit
> there is in being serviceable. Get your voice disciplined
> and clear, and think only of accuracy. If you have any
> soul worth expressing it will show itself in your singing.
> --Ruskin

Ernestine Schumann-Heink's Metropolitan Opera debut took place on January 9, 1899, in "Lohengrin."

First performance in America of Dvorak's Second Symphony
was played by the New York Philharmonic on January 9,
1886, under the direction of Theodore Thomas.

Rudolf Bing was born January 9, 1902.

John Knowles Paine was born January 9, 1839.

Julian Gayarre was born January 9, 1844.

January Tenth

> The quality which Chopin most valued in the player was
> a sympathetic touch. --Williby

Walter Gieseking's first American Concert took place at
Town Hall in New York City on January 10, 1926.

Premiere performance of Vincent D'Indy's "Istor Variations"
was given simultaneously, January 10, 1897, by William Mengelberg in Amsterdam and Eugene Ysaye in Brussels.

Benjamin Godard died January 10, 1895.

John Brownlee died January 10, 1969.

January Eleventh

> A singer who is not able to recite his part according to
> the intention of the poet cannot possibly sing it according
> to the intention of the composer. --Wagner

Lotte Lehman made her Metropolitan Opera debut on January
11, 1934, in "Die Walkure."

Metropolitan premiere of "The Magic Flute" took place on
January 11, 1904, with Marcella Sembrich and Milka Ternina
in the cast.

Marcella Sembrich died January 11, 1935.

American debut of Egon Petri took place on January 11, 1932.

Reinhold Gliere was born January 11, 1875.

First performance of Aaron Copland's Symphony for Organ and Orchestra was played by the New York Symphony Society on January 11, 1925.

January Twelfth

> There is sweet music here that softer falls
> Than petals from blown roses on the grass,
> Or night-dews on still waters between walls
> Of shadowy granite, in a gleaming pass;
> Music that gentler on the spirit lies
> Than tired eyelids upon tired eyes. --Tennyson

American debut of Vladimir Horowitz took place on January 12, 1928, with the New York Philharmonic under Sir Thomas Beecham, who was also making his first appearance in America.

Ermanno Wolf-Ferrari was born January 12, 1876.

Arabella Goddard was born January 12, 1836.

Francesca Cuzzoni made her debut as Teofane in Handel's opera "Ottone" on January 12, 1723.

Metropolitan permiere of Rossini's opera "Semiramide" was on January 12, 1894, with Nellie Melba, Sofia Scalchi and Edouard de Reszke heading the cast.

Town Hall in New York City opened on January 12, 1925.

Leopold Ludwig was born January 12, 1908.

January Thirteenth

> Listen attentively to all folk-songs: these are a treasure
> of lovely melodies, and will teach you the characteristics
> of different nations. --Schumann

Stephen Foster died January 13, 1864.

Ferdinand Ries died January 13, 1838.

American debut of Rudolf Firkusny took place January 13, 1938, in Town Hall, New York.

Charles Kullman was born January 13, 1903.

Metropolitan Opera debut of Leonard Warren was presented January 13, 1939.

Heinrich Hoffmann was born January 13, 1842.

First performance of "Sleeping Beauty," ballet by Peter Ilyich Tchaikowsky, was presented January 13, 1890, in St. Petersburg.

January Fourteenth

> Study only the best, for life is too short to study everything. --Emanuel Bach

Madame Malibran,
the "Siren of Europe,"
died in 1836 at the age of 28.

Albert Schweitzer was born January 14, 1875.

First performance of "La Tosca" was produced in Rome, January 14, 1900, at the Teatro Constanzi. Leopoldo Mugnone conducted the world premiere.

Stephen Heller died January 14, 1888.

Maria Malibran made her Parisian operatic debut on January 14, 1828.

Jean De Reszke, reigning tenor of the last "Golden Age," was born January 14, 1850.

Last concert of Anton Rubinstein took place in St. Petersburg on January 14, 1894.

January Fifteenth

> Talent is a power which exists independent of human aid, the want of which no teacher can supply. It is that power which makes itself felt in the performance of those influencing us with an irrestible force.--Merz

Metropolitan premiere of "Louise" with Geraldine Farrar on January 15, 1921.

Luisa Tetrazzini made her New York debut in "La Traviata" on January 15, 1908.

Dimitri Mitropoulos led the world premiere of Samuel Barber's "Vanessa" on January 15, 1958, at the Metropolitan Opera in New York.

Ruth Slenczynski was born January 15, 1925.

Metropolitan premiere of "Mefistofele" was given on January 15, 1896, with Emma Calvé and Edouard de Reszke in the cast.

January Sixteenth

> Artists will derive additional facility of execution from
> hearing and cultivating vocal as well as instrumental
> music. --C. P. E. Bach

Metropolitan debut of Frida Leider took place on January 16,
1933, as Isolde.

Arturo Toscanini died January 16, 1957.

Metropolitan premiere of "Manon" took place on January 16,
1895, with Sybil Sanderson, Jean de Reszke, Mario Ancona
and Pol Plancon.

London debut of pianist Katharine Goodson took place on January 16, 1897.

Leo Delibes died January 16, 1891.

The first Metropolitan performance of "Zaza" was given on
January 16, 1920, with Geraldine Farrar, Pasquale Amato
and Giulio Crimi.

Amilcare Ponchielli died January 16, 1886.

January Seventeenth

> In the works of Beethoven are to be found gigantic and
> sublime formulae; those of Haydn contain a melodic
> sweetness mixed with artifices which are always agree-
> able; while Mozart showed his unequaled genius in every-
> thing.   I can only compare them to Michaelangelo,
> Guida, and Raphael. --Pacini

Wilhelm Kienzl was born January 17, 1857.

Ignaz Jan Paderewski became Premier of Poland on January
17, 1919.

World premiere of the opera, "Il Maschere," by Pietro Mascagni, was given simultaneously in seven cities on January
17, 1901.

January Eighteenth

Always play as if a master heard you. --<u>Schumann</u>

American debut of the English pianist, Katharine Goodson, took place on January 18, 1907.

Puccini's "Manon Lescaut" was presented at the Metropolitan Opera House for the first time on January 18, 1907, under the personal direction of the composer. In the cast were Enrico Caruso, Lina Cavalieri and Antonio Scotti.

Emanuel Chabrier was born January 18, 1841.

Abram Chasins made his formal concert debut by performing his own first concerto on January 18, 1929, with the Philadelphia Orchestra. Ossip Gabrilowitsch conducted.

Joseph Tichatschek, Bohemian tenor who created the roles of "Rienzi" and "Tannhauser, " died January 18, 1886.

Jan Smeterlin died January 18, 1967.

Berthold Goldschmidt was born January 18, 1903.

January Nineteenth

The mind which is not gifted with the powers of imagination may be fitted for other studies than music, but in the arts it will always be dull and inert. --<u>Merz</u>

World premiere of "Il Trovatore" took place on January 19, 1853, at the Teatro Apollo in Rome.

When Titta Ruffo reached the Metropolitan Opera House as a member of the company, on the night of January 19, 1922, in Rossini's "Barbiere di Siviglia, " he arrived as the most famous baritone of his era.

Massenet's "Manon" was presented at the Opera Comique in Paris for the world premiere performance on January 19, 1884.

Albert Louis Wolff was born January 19, 1884.

Hans Sachs died at Nuremberg on January 19, 1576.

Hans Hotter was born January 19, 1909.

January Twentieth

> Respect the pianoforte! It gives a single man command
> over something complete; in its ability to go from very
> soft to very loud in one and the same register it excels
> all other instruments. The trumpet can blare, but not
> sigh; the flute is the contrary; the pianoforte can do
> both. Its range embraces the highest and lowest prac-
> ticable notes. Respect the pianoforte!--<u>Busoni</u>

Josef Hofmann was born January 20, 1876.

Robert Casadesus made his American debut on January 20,
1935, as soloist of the New York Philharmonic Symphony
Society, Hans Lange conducting in the Mozart Coronation
Concerto.

Wilhelmine Schroder-Devrient, just sixteen, made her opera
debut on January 20, 1821, as Pamina in "The Magic Flute."

Walter Piston was born January 20, 1894.

Mischa Elman was born January 20, 1891.

Gertrud Elisabeth Mara died January 20, 1833.

Antonio Scotti gave his Metropolitan farewell performance on
January 20, 1933.

January Twenty-first

> Art is in man what creative power is in God.--<u>Abbe de
> Lamennais</u>

Erich Leinsdorf's Metropolitan debut as conductor took place
January 21, 1938.

Euphrosyne Parepa-Rosa died January 21, 1874.

Ernest Chausson was born January 21, 1855.

First performance of Maria Luigi Cherubini's "Requiem" was
given on January 21, 1816, in Paris.

Albert Lortzing died January 21, 1851.

Ermanno Wolf-Ferrari died January 21, 1948.

January Twenty-second

As you grow older, converse more with scores than
with virtuosos. --Schumann

Rosa Ponselle was born January 22, 1897.

The first Metropolitan performance of "Salome" was presented on January 22, 1907, with Olive Fremstad as Salome.

Brahms' Concerto No. I, for piano and orchestra was introduced in Hanover on January 22, 1859, with Brahms playing
the solo part and Joseph Joachim conducting the orchestra.

Adolf Brodsky died January 22, 1929.

World premiere of Stravinsky's First Symphony was presented January 22, 1908, in St. Petersburg.

January Twenty-third

And while we hear
The tides of Music's golden sea
Setting toward eternity,
Uplifted high in heart and hope are we. --Tennyson

American premiere of "La Traviata" took place at the Metropolitan Opera on January 23, 1909, with Marcella Sembrich
and Enrico Caruso.

Muzio Clementi was born January 23, 1752.

Serge Koussevitzky's conducting debut took place on January
23, 1908, with the Berlin Philharmonic.

Edward Mac Dowell died January 23, 1908.

John Field died January 23, 1837.

Luigi Lablache died January 23, 1858.

January Twenty-fourth

Music is well said to be the speech of angels.--Carlyle

"I Puritani" was first produced at the Theatre des Italiens in Paris with Giulia Grisi and Giovanni Battista Rubini on January 24, 1835. It created a great furore. Bellini wrote afterwards: "The whole stage was flooded with bouquets." Rossini proclaimed it Bellini's greatest work.

The Metropolitan presented the young Australian soprano, Marjorie Lawrence, in "Alceste" on January 24, 1941.

Carlo Farinelli, possibly the greatest of all singers of his day, was born January 24, 1705.

E. T. A. Hoffmann was born January 24, 1776.

Otto Klemperer made his bow in America on January 24, 1926, when he appeared as a guest of the New York Symphony Society.

Norman Dello Joio was born January 24, 1913.

The Royal Philharmonic Society of London was founded January 24, 1813.

Leon Kirchner was born January 24, 1919.

Edwin Fischer died January 24, 1960.

William Mason was born January 24, 1829.

Gasparo Spontini died January 24, 1851.

Friedrich Von Flotow died January 24, 1883.

January Twenty-fifth

        Do you not recall
        How the words fitted to the melody--
        A carol joyous as it spread its wings,
        And falling into minors at its close?--
                              Francis Howard Williams

Antonio Scotti was born January 25, 1866.

Metropolitan debut of Richard Tucker as Enzo in "La Gioconda" took place on January 25, 1945.

Ettore Bastianini died January 25, 1967.

The first Metropolitan performance of "Die Götterdämmerung" was presented on January 25, 1888, with Anton Seidl conducting.

World premiere of "Elektra" was produced on January 25, 1909, in Dresden.   Ernst von Schuch conducted.

Maestro Wilhelm Furtwangler was born January 25, 1886.

Peter Klein was born January 25, 1907.

January Twenty-sixth

> Every note of Mozart's is a round in the ladder of the spheres, by which he ascended to the heaven of perfection. --Jean Paul Richter

First performance of Mozart's "Cosi Fan Tutti" was given at the Burgtheatre in Vienna on January 26, 1790.

"Der Rosenkavalier" was first produced on January 26, 1911, in Dresden with Ernst von Schuch conducting.

Vaughan Williams' "Pastoral Symphony" was first performed January 26, 1922, by the Royal Philharmonic Society in London under Sir Adrian Boult.

Poulenc's "Les Dialogues de Carmélites" was first performed on January 26, 1957, at La Scala in Milan with Nino Sanzogno conducting.

Wilhelmine Schroder-Devrient died January 26, 1860.

Grace Moore died in an airplane crash in Copenhagen on January 26, 1947.

Ignaz Friedman died January 26, 1948.

January Twenty-seventh

> From whatever side and with whatever feeling we may
> glance at Mozart, we always meet with the genuine and
> pure nature of the artist, a nature filled with perennial
> love, which finds only joy and satisfaction in producing
> the beautiful, animated with the spirit of truth. --Jahn

Wolfgang Amadeus Mozart,
born January 27, 1756.

Wolfgang Amadeus Mozart was born January 27, 1756.

Giuseppe Verdi died January 27, 1901.

On January 27, 1959, Maria Callas sang the role of Imogene
in a concert performance of "Il Pirata" at Carnegie Hall,
New York, under the auspices of the American Opera Society.

Memorable performance of "Don Giovanni" in honor of Mozart's birth, at the Metropolitan, New York, on January 27,
1906, with Lillian Nordica, Marcella Sembrich and Antonio
Scotti.

The debut of Leontyne Price and Franco Corelli took place at the Metropolitan Opera House on January 27, 1961, in 'Il Trovatore."

Josef Lhevinne made his American debut in New York on January 27, 1906.

John Ogdon was born January 27, 1937.

Edouard Lalo was born January 27, 1823.

Paul Kalisch died January 27, 1946.

Erich Kleiber died January 27, 1956.

First performance of Tippett's opera "The Midsummer Marriage" took place on January 27, 1955, at Covent Garden, London. John Pritchard conducted the premiere; the principal roles were taken by Joan Sutherland, Adele Leigh and Monica Sinclair.

Cesari Siepi made his American debut at the Metropolitan Opera on January 27, 1951.

Manuel Del Popolo Garcia was born January 27, 1775.

Bartolommeo Cristofori died January 27, 1731.

January Twenty-eighth

> If the composer can only move the imaginative power of his hearers, and call forth some one image, some one thought--it matters not what--he has attained his object.
> --Mendelssohn

Artur Rubinstein was born January 28, 1886.

Amelita Galli-Curci made her triumphant New York debut in Meyerbeer's "Le Pardon de Ploermel" on January 28, 1918. Cleofonte Campanini conducted.

Victor Nessler was born January 28, 1841.

Metropolitan premiere performance of "Ernani" took place on January 28, 1903, with Marcella Sembrich, Antonio Scotti and Edouard de Reszke in the cast.

American premiere of Verdi's "Simon Boccanegra" was present-
ed on January 28, 1932, at the Metropolitan Opera in New York.
Tullio Serafin conducted and the cast included Lawrence Tibbett,
Giovanni Martinelli, Ezio Pinza and Maria Müller.

Michael Ippolitoff-Ivanoff died January 28, 1935.

World premiere of Leonard Bernstein's "Jeremiah" was given
on January 28, 1944, by the Pittsburgh Symphony Orchestra
under the direction of the composer.

Emmy Destinn died February 9, 1960.

January Twenty-ninth

> Reverence the old, but meet the new also with a warm
> heart.   Cherish no prejudice against names unknown to
> you. --Schumann

Frederick Delius was born January 29, 1862.

Sir Frederic Cowen was born January 29, 1852.

Metropolitan premiere of "Le Pardon de Ploërmel" was
given on January 29, 1892.

Maria Müller was born January 29, 1898.

January Thirtieth

> There's music in the sighing of a reed
> There's music in the gushing of a rill;
> There's music in all things, if men had ears:
> Their earth is but an echo of the spheres. --
>
> Byron

Francis Poulenc died January 30, 1963.

Weber's debut as conductor at the Dresden Opera took place
on January 30, 1817.

Walter Damrosch was born January 30, 1862.

Robert Casadesus appeared with Toscanini in Brahms B Flat
Major Concerto on January 30, 1936.

Metropolitan premiere of "Die Walküre" was presented on January 30, 1885, under Leopold Damrosch.

Charles Martin Loeffler was born January 30, 1861.

January Thirty-first

> There was a time when I talked unwillingly of Schubert, whose name, I thought, should only be whispered at night to the trees and stars. --Schumann

Franz Schubert,
born January 31, 1797.

Franz Peter Schubert was born January 31, 1797.

Metropolitan debut of Renata Tebaldi took place on January 31, 1955.

"Le Nozze di Figaro" was first heard at the Metropolitan Opera on January 31, 1894, with Lillian Nordica, Emma Eames, Mario Ancona and Edouard de Reszke.

A master returns to Opera! Giovanni Martinelli sang the
role of the Chinese emperor in Puccini's "Turandot" on January 31, 1967.   This was his first appearance on an operatic
stage in seventeen years.

FEBRUARY

I can always leave off talking when
I hear a master play. --Browning

February First

There is fame enough for one man in the 'Overture to
A Midsummer Night's Dream' of Mendelssohn. --
Schumann

Mendelssohn was just seventeen when he wrote the remarkable "Overture to A Midsummer Night's Dream." The first
public performance took place at Stettin in February, 1827,
with Karl Lowe conducting from manuscript.

Renata Tebaldi, one of the reigning prima donnas of the Metropolitan Opera, was born February 1, 1922.

World premiere of Puccini's "La Bohème" took place at the
Teatro Regio in Turin on February 1, 1896, with Arturo
Toscanini conducting.

Annette Essipoff was born February 1, 1851.

Victor Herbert was born February 1, 1859.

"Manon Lescaut" by Puccini was heard for the first time on
February 1, 1893, at the Teatro Regio in Turin.

February Second

Palestrina's music has all its separate parts so beautiful
that one would like to sing them all one's self. --
Hauptmann

Giovanni Palestrina died February 2, 1594.

Isabella Colbran was born February 2, 1785.

Fritz Kreisler was born February 2, 1875.

Jasha Heifetz was born February 2, 1901.

First performance of Charpentier's "Louise" was given at the Opera Comique in Paris on February 2, 1900.

Kirsten Flagstad made her Metropolitan debut on February 2, 1935, in "Die Walkure." The evening was a sensation.

Jussi Bjorling was born February 2, 1911.

Girolama Crescentini, one of the last and finest of the Italian artificial mezzo-sopranos, was born February 2, 1762.

John Charles Thomas made his Metropolitan debut on February 2, 1934.

Premiere of "Fluchtversuch" by Boris Blacher was presented February 2, 1966, at the Hamburg Opera.

Giovanni Martinelli died February 2, 1969.

Maestro Tulio Serafin died February 2, 1968.

Lisa Della Casa was born February 2, 1919.

February Third

> It is not his (Mendelssohn's) genius that surprises me and compels my admiration, for that he has from God. No, it is his incessant toil, his bee-like industry, his stern conscientiousness, his inflexibility toward himself, his actual adoration of Art. --Zelter

Felix Mendelssohn-Bartholdy was born February 3, 1809.

World premiere of Rossini's "Semiramide" took place at the Fenice Theatre in Venice on February 3, 1823.

Luigi Dallapiccola was born February 3, 1904.

Giulio Gatti-Casazza, director of the Metropolitan Opera House, New York (1908-1935), was born February 3, 1869.

Felix Mendelssohn-Bartholdy,
born February 3, 1809.

February Fourth

   The road to perfection, to mastership, lies in the direction of constant application. --Merz

Maestro Erich Leinsdorf was born February 4, 1912.

The first New York performance of "La Tosca" was produced at the Metropolitan Opera on February 4, 1901. In
the cast were Antonio Scotti and Milka Ternina.

Claudio Arrau made his American debut playing with the
Boston Symphony on February 4, 1924.

Metropolitan premiere of "Falstaff" took place February 4,
1895, with Victor Maurel and Emma Eames.

Fritz Reiner made his Metropolitan debut on February 4,

1949, in a performance of Richard Strauss' "Salome."

February Fifth

What shall I say of Jenny Lind? This wonderful artiste
stands far too high in my estimation to be dragged down
by commonplace phrases such as newspaper writers so
copiously indulge in. --Moscheles

Jenny Lind and Otto Goldschmidt were married February 5,
1852.

"Otello" was first performed on February 5, 1887, at La
Scala in Milan with Francesco Tamagno and Victor Maurel
in the cast.

Rosina Lhevinne made her debut with the Moscow Symphony
Orchestra on February 5, 1895.

Metropolitan premiere of Wagner's "Rienzi" took place on
February 5, 1886, when Anton Seidl conducted a distinguished
cast including Marianne Brandt, Lilli Lehmann and Emil Fischer.

Ludwig Thuille died February 5, 1907.

John Pritchard was born February 5, 1921.

Ole Bull was born at Bergen on February 5, 1810.

February Sixth

The aesthetic principle is the same in every art; only
the material differs. --Schumann

Marcella Sembrich bade farewell to the operatic stage of
America on February 6, 1909.

Claudio Arrau was born February 6, 1903.

World premiere performance of Schumann's Third Symphony
was given in Dusseldorf on February 6, 1851, with the composer conducting.

Julie Dorus-Gras died February 6, 1896.

rformance of his "Emperor Concerto" on February

erkin made his debut on February 12, 1937, playing
n's "Emperor Concerto" with the Philadelphia Or-

Bulow died February 12, 1894.

ris was born February 12, 1898.

's "Rhapsody in Blue" was first performed in New
February 12, 1924, with Paul Whiteman conducting
composer as soloist.

Ambroise Thomas died February 12, 1896.

Zeffirelli was born February 12, 1923.

Thirteenth

understanding is not a vessel which must be filled,
irewood, which needs to be kindled; and love of
ing and love of truth are what should kindle it.--
rch

Wagner died February 13, 1883.

Godowsky was born February 13, 1870.

utiful Blue Danube Waltz" by Johann Strauss was
the first time on February 13, 1867, in Vienna.

rgmuller died February 13, 1874.

esi was born February 13, 1700.

miere of Handel's "Rodelinda" was on February 13,
London.

rrell was born February 13, 1920.

anovitch Chaliapin was born February 13, 1873.

February Seventh

Natural gift may produce a poet, but it does not make a
musician. The highest perfection is reached only by un-
tiring practice and almost ceaseless work.--F. Brendel

Ossip Gabrilowitch was born February 7, 1878.

Metropolitan debut of Grace Moore took place on February 7,
1928.

Jan Smeterlin was born February 7, 1892.

The Cleveland Orchestra under George Szell presented the
New York premiere of Busoni's Piano Concerto (with male
chorus) on February 7, 1966, at Carnegie Hall.

Quincy Porter was born February 7, 1897.

First performance of "Peter Ibbetson," opera by Deems
Taylor, was given on February 7, 1931, at the Metropolitan
Opera in New York.

Claudia Muzio was born February 7, 1889.

February Eighth

It is art and science alone that reveal to us and give us
the hope of a loftier life.--Beethoven

Italian premiere of "Aida" took place at La Scala in Milan
on February 8, 1872. Teresa Stolz sang the name role.

Vincenzo Bellezza, noted operatic conductor, died February
8, 1964.

World premiere of "Boris Godounov" took place on February
8, 1874, at the Imperial Opera House in St. Petersburg.

February Ninth

It is not enough for us to be musicians only. We must
be men and women of general information, of liberal ed-
ucation--in short, men and women of culture.--Gates

Ernst von Dohnanyi died February 9, 1960.

World premiere performance of "The Beggar's Opera" was given in London February 9, 1728.

Johann Ludwig Dussek was born February 9, 1761.

World premiere of Verdi's "Falstaff" took place at La Scala in Milan on February 9, 1893. At the composer's request, Edoardo Mascheroni conducted.

Licia Albanese made her bow at the Metropolitan Opera February 9, 1940, as Cio-Cio-San in "Madame Butterfly."

Alban Berg was born February 9, 1885.

February Tenth

Music, once admitted to the soul, becomes a sort of spirit, and never dies.--Bulwer

Adelina Patti,
born February 10, 1843.

Adelina Patti, one of the most was born February 10, 1843.

Leontyne Price was born Febru

First American performance of was given on February 10, 184

Cesare Siepi was born Februar

Offenbach's "Les Contes d' Hof February 10, 1881, in Paris.

Concerto No. 20 in D minor, piano concertos, was first perf

February Eleventh

What can wake the soul's world like music?--L. E.

American premiere of Puccini place at the Metropolitan Oper Farrar, Enrico Caruso, Anton February 11, 1907. Puccini performance conducted by Art

Rudolf Firkusny was born Feb

First performance of Verdi's at La Scala on February 11, the Giselda of the world prem

Percy Grainger made his Am February 11, 1915, in New Y

First performance of Anton given February 11, 1903, in

February Twelfth

It is one thing to give ou another to yield to inspi

Beethoven was present when

nese pe
12, 181

Rudolf S
Beethove
chestra.

Hans vo

Roy Har

Gershwi
York on
and the

Charles

Franco

February

The
but
learr
Pluta

Richard

Leopold

"The Bea
heard for

Johann B

Vittoria

World pr
1725, in

Eileen Fa

Feodor Iv

February Fourteenth

> Genius at first is a little more than a great capacity
> for receiving discipline. --George Eliot

Prokofieff conducted his own "The Love for Three Oranges"
at the Metropolitan Opera in New York on February 14, 1922.

Ignaz Friedman was born February 14, 1882.

First performance of Alexander Borodin's Symphony No. 2
took place at St. Petersburg on February 14, 1877.

World premiere of Bellini's "La Staniera" was given February 14, 1829, with Henriette Meric-Lalande, Antonio Tamburini and Caroline Unger.

Bruno Walter was heard for the first time at the Metropolitan Opera, making his debut there on February 14, 1941, in
Beethoven's "Fidelio."

Handel became a British subject, swearing allegiance to
George I on February 1, 1727.

Handel and George I on the Thames.

February Fifteenth

> Have you real talent for art? Then study music, do
> something worthy of the art, and dedicate your whole
> soul to the beloved saint. --Longfellow

Marcella Sembrich was born February 15, 1858.

Bruno Walter made his American debut by appearing as a
guest conductor of the New York Symphony Society on February 15, 1923.

As Tosca, Emma Eames made her farewell to the Metropolitan Opera on February 15, 1909.

American debut of Joseph Krips as a symphony conductor
was with the Buffalo Philharmonic on February 15, 1953.

Michael Glinka died February 15, 1857.

Michael Praetorius was born February 15, 1571, and died
February 15, 1621.

Frederick Ernst was born February 15, 1789.

The American Music Center was founded on February 15,
1940, in New York City.

Henry E. Steinway was born February 15, 1797.

Leopold Damrosch died February 15, 1885.

February Sixteenth

> Many critics mistake the rules of the theory of music
> for the rules by which to criticize the beautiful in it. --
> Merz

Liszt performed Wagner's "Tannhauser" at Weimar on February 16, 1849.

Chopin gave his last concert for a Paris audience on February 16, 1848.

Philipp Scharwenka was born February 16, 1847.

Alexander Brailowsky was born February 16, 1896.

Josef Hofmann died February 16, 1957.

Metropolitan premiere of "Thais" took place February 16, 1917, with Geraldine Farrar, Luca Botta and Pasquale Amato.

Fernando Previtali was born February 16, 1907.

Geraint Evans was born February 16, 1922.

David Mannes was born February 16, 1866.

February Seventeenth

> Genius is the most beautiful gift with which nature favors mankind from time to time.   Through it we are allowed to enjoy what is most sublime--self-oblivion in a loftier life.--F. Hiller

Joan Sutherland soared to international fame after her performance of Lucia at the Royal Opera House, Covent Garden on February 17, 1959.   Tullio Serafin conducted.

Puccini's "Madame Butterfly" was first heard February 17, 1904, at La Scala in Milan.   Rosina Storchio sang the title role.

The first performance of Liszt's Piano Concerto in E Flat Major was given on February 17, 1855, at the palace of the Grand Duke in Weimar with the composer at the piano and Von Bulow conducting.

Lauritz Melchoir made his debut on February 17, 1926, in "Tannhauser" at the Metropolitan Opera.

The Teatro Apollo in Rome was the scene of the first performance of "Un Ballo in Maschero" on February 17, 1859.

Marion Anderson was born February 17, 1902.

Arcangelo Corelli was born February 17, 1653.

Marjorie Lawrence was born February 17, 1909.

Lee Hoiby was born February 17, 1926.

Vincenzo Bellezza was born February 17, 1888.

Geoffrey Toye was born February 17, 1889.

February Eighteenth

Paganini is the turning-point of virtuosity. --Schumann

Niccolo Paganini,
born February 18, 1784.
Portrait by Maurin.

A German Requiem, by Johannes Brahms, was first performed on February 18, 1869, in Leipzig with Karl Reinecke
conducting.

First performance of the opera "La Damnation de Faust" by
Berlioz was given in Monte Carlo on February 18, 1893.
Jean de Reszke was the Faust of the world premiere.

Handel's oratorio "Samson" was first performed at Covent Garden Theatre on February 18, 1743.

Dimitri Mitropoulos was born February 18, 1896.

Maestro Bruno Walter died February 18, 1962.

Music publisher, Gustave Schirmer, was born February 18, 1864.

Brigitta Banti died February 18, 1806.

Gustave Charpentier died February 18, 1956.

February Nineteenth

> The soul of Music is of the Spirit, and her mind is of the Heart. --Kahlil Gibran

Joan Sutherland made her Italian debut at the Teatro La Fenice in Venice on February 19, 1960, in a most spectacular performance of Handel's "Alcina."

Luigi Boccherini was born February 19, 1743.

American premiere of "Pelleas et Melisande," winning acclaim for Mary Garden at the Manhattan Opera, New York on February 19, 1908.

Giovanni Pacini was born February 19, 1796.

Maestro Joseph Krips' Metropolitan Opera debut, conducting his favorite opera "The Magic Flute" at New York's new Metropolitan Opera House, took place on February 19, 1967.

American premiere of "The Bartered Bride" took place at the Metropolitan Opera with Emmy Destinn and Adamo Didur on February 19, 1909.

Tobias Matthay was born February 19, 1858.

February Twentieth

> If in spite of all the abuse and ill treatment to which it is subjected the noble art of music never ceases to charm and edify us, it only attests its unfathomable and everlasting grandeur. --Ferdinand Hiller

Handel's opera "Giulo Cesare" was first produced at the King's Theatre in the Haymarket on February 20, 1724.

Mary Garden was born February 20, 1877.

The first performance of Rossini's "Il Barbiere di Siviglia" was given in Rome at the Teatro di Torre Argentina on February 20, 1816, with the composer conducting.

Karl Czerny was born February 20, 1791.

Henri Vieuxtemps was born February 20, 1820.

Isidor Philipp died February 20, 1958.

Ferenc Fricsay died February 20, 1963.

Ernest Ansermet, founder of L'Orchestre de la Suisse Romande, died February 20, 1969.

February Twenty-first

'Who sings?' said the Spirit of Music,
    And smiled on her peers:
'Sweet Sorrow, sing thou!' Sorrow answered,
    'I cannot--for tears.'
'Bright Hope, give a tongue to the poems
    I read in thine eyes.'
Hope answered--'My thoughts are all clouded
    And lost in the skies.'
'Then Joy, put thy mouth to the bugle!
    A note for my sake.'
Calm creature, she sleeps in the sunshine,
    And will not awake.
But hush! a soft sound stealeth onwards
    Like the flight of a dove;
Ah, I find that the Song that is sweetest,
    Comes ever from Love.--

                                 Cornwall

Joan Sutherland made her New York debut in a concert performance of Bellini's opera "Beatrice di Tenda" at Town Hall on February 21, 1961. Nicola Rescigno conducted.

Leo Delibes was born February 21, 1836.

John Pyke Hullah died February 21, 1884.

Theodore Doehler died February 21, 1856.

First performance in America of "Feste di Roma," symphonic poem by Ottorino Respighi, was given in New York on
February 21, 1929, under the direction of Arturo Toscanini.

February Twenty-second

> He (Chopin) confided....those inexpressible sorrows to
> which the pious gave vent in their communication with
> their Maker.   What they never say except upon their
> knees, he said in his palpitating compositions.--Liszt

Frederic Chopin was born February 22, 1810.

Benno Moiseiwitsch was born February 22, 1890.

Tchaikowsky's Symphony No. 4 was first performed on February 22, 1878, in Moscow.

Niels Wilhelm Gade was born February 22, 1817.

Hugo Wolf died February 22, 1903.

Metropolitan debut of Ramon Vinay took place on February
22, 1946.

Robert Weede was born February 22, 1903.

American music critic, Irving Kolodin, was born February
22, 1908.

Mario Ancona died February 22, 1931.

Johanna Gadski died February 22, 1932.

February Twenty-third

> Handel is the unequaled master of all masters.   Go,
> turn to him and learn, with few means, how to produce
> such great effects.--Beethoven

George Frederic Handel was born February 23, 1685.

"La Juive" (Halevy) was first performed February 23, 1835.

Nellie Melba died February 23, 1931.

Gertrud Elisabeth Mara, the first German soprano to achieve and sustain a career of international fame, was born February 23, 1740.

Sophie Mentor died February 23, 1918.

First performance of Symphonic Poem No. 3 "Les Preludes" by Franz Liszt was given February 23, 1854.

Sir Edward Elgar died February 23, 1934.

February Twenty-fourth

> Why music was ordained?
> Was it not to refresh the mind of man
> After his studies, or his usual pain?
> Then give me leave to read philosophy
> And while I pause serve in your harmony.--
>
> Shakespeare

First performance of Monteverdi's opera "Orfeo" was given February 24, 1607, in Mantua.

World premiere of Handel's first opera "Rinaldo" was presented on February 24, 1711, in London at the Queens Theatre. The cast was superb. It included Giuseppe Maria Boschi and Nicolini.

Johann Baptist Cramer was born February 24, 1771.

Ibsen's "Peer Gynt" with Grieg's music was first produced on February 24, 1876, at Christiania (Oslo).

Frederic Chopin, at eight years of age, gave his first concert February 24, 1818, at the Radziwell palace.

Rudolph Ganz was born February 24, 1877.

Andre Messager died February 24, 1929.

Arrigo Boito was born February 24, 1842.

Chopin at Prince Radziwell's--
from a painting by H. Siemiradski.

February Twenty-fifth

Fancy and feeling go naturally together, and, indeed,
ought to be united; but such union is rare, and is one
of the surest signs of genius.--Pauer

Enrico Caruso was born February 25, 1873.

Myra Hess was born February 25, 1890.

Richard Crooks made his Metropolitan debut as de Grieux in
"Manon" on February 25, 1933.

Anton Arensky died February 25, 1906.

Thomas Moore died February 25, 1852.

Puccini was seriously injured in an automobile accident, February 25, 1903.

Armand Louis Couperin was born February 25, 1725.

American debut of Alice Ehlers at Town Hall in New York
took place on February 25, 1936.

February Twenty-sixth

> Softness of touch depends on keeping the fingers as
> close as possible to the keys. --F. Couperin

American debut of Clifford Curzon took place on February
26, 1939, in New York.

Antonio Scotti died February 26, 1936.

Emmy Destinn was born February 26, 1878.

Frederic Chopin made his Paris debut as a pianist on February 26, 1832.

Giuseppe Tartini died February 26, 1770.

February Twenty-seventh

> It is in music, perhaps, that the soul most nearly at-
> tains the great end for which, when inspired by the
> poetic sentiment, it struggles--the creation of supernal
> beauty. --Edgar Allen Poe

Beethoven's "Eighth Symphony" was first performed February
27, 1814, in Vienna.

Lotte Lehmann was born February 27, 1888.

Alexander Borodin died February 27, 1887.

Mary Garden sang the role of "Aphrodite" at the American
premiere in the Metropolitan Opera on February 27, 1920.
Edward Johnson, in his first season at "the Met," supported
her.

Joseph Victor Capoul was born February 27, 1839.

February Twenty-eighth

> Art is a grateful friend....the more one devotes to her,
> the greater return she makes. --Leschetizky, in a letter
> to Ethel Newcomb

Ethel Newcomb made her debut on February 28, 1903, with the Vienna Philharmonic Orchestra.

Geraldine Farrar was born February 28, 1882.

Guiomar Novaes was born February 28, 1895.

D'Indy's Second Symphony, in B-flat, was first performed at a Lamoureux concert in Paris, February 28, 1904.

Pauline Lucca died February 28, 1915.

William Lichtenwanger was born February 28, 1915.

The Royal College of Music in London was founded on February 28, 1882.

Amy Fay died February 28, 1928.

Mario Ancona was born February 28, 1860.

First performances of Roy Harris's Second Symphony and Prelude and Fugue for Strings was presented by the Boston Symphony Orchestra and Philadelphia Symphony Orchestra respectively on February 28, 1936.

February Twenty-ninth

> Art in general is that magic instrumentality by which man's mind reveals to man's senses that great mystery, the beautiful. --Ritter

Gioacchino Rossini was born February 29, 1792.

Opening night of Meyerbeer's "Les Huguenots" was on February 29, 1836 in Paris. The cast included Cornelie Falcon, Julie Dorus-Gras, Adolphe Nourrit and Nicholas Levasseur.

Gioacchino Rossini,
born February 29, 1792.

MARCH

Music to the mind, is as
air to the body. --Plato

March First

True virtuosity gives us something more than mere
flexibility and execution. A man may mirror his own
nature in his playing. --Schumann

Girolamo Frescobaldi died March 1, 1643.

Ebenezer Prout was born March 1, 1835.

Theodore Kullak died March 1, 1882.

Dimitr Mitropoulos was born March 1, 1896.

World premiere of Pizzetti's "Assassinio Nella Cattedrale"
took place at La Scala in Milan on March 1, 1958. Gianandrea Gavazzeni conducted.

March Second

Were it not for music we might in these days say the
beautiful is dead. --D'Israeli

Giovanni Rubini, the darling of La Scala, died March 2, 1854.

Emma Calvé sang a last Carmen on March 2, 1904, at the
Metropolitan Opera House in New York.

Friederich Smetana was born March 2, 1824.

Marc Blitzstein was born March 2, 1905.

Bernhardt Breitkopf, founder of the music publishing firm in
Leipzig, was born March 2, 1695.

47

Kurt Weill was born March 2, 1900.

March Third

> All music is an idealization of the natural language of
> passion. --Herbert Spencer

Brahms' Alto Rhapsody, written for Pauline Viardot, was
first sung by her on March 3, 1870.

Premiere performance of The Scotch Symphony of Mendelssohn was presented on March 3, 1842, at the Leipzig Gwendhaus with the composer conducting.

Bizet's "Carmen" was given its first performance at the
Opera Comique in Paris on March 3, 1875.   Celestine Galli-
Marie was the Carmen of the world premiere.

Eugene D'Albert died March 3, 1932.

Sir Henry Wood was born March 3, 1869.

First Metropolitan performance of Menotti's "Amelia Goes
to the Ball" was given on March 3, 1938.

English debut of Bruno Walter took place on March 3, 1909.

Paul Wittgenstein died March 3, 1961.

James Friskin was born March 3, 1886.

Adolphe Nourrit was born March 3, 1802.

Academie des Operas was inaugurated March 3, 1671, in
Paris.

Feodor Chaliapin gave his last recital in New York City on
March 3, 1935.

March Fourth

> The noisiest and most complicated music has melody,
> but it may be so laden with external flourishes, or so
> obscured by internal changes, that few only can detect
> and follow the golden thread. --Christiani

Serge Prokofiev died March 4, 1953.

The first oratorio presentation of "Parsifal" in America occurred on March 4, 1886, at the Metropolitan Opera under
Walter Damrosch with Marianne Brandt and Emil Fischer.

Leonard Warren died March 4, 1960.

Moritz Moszkowski died in Paris on March 4, 1925.

Henry Colles died March 4, 1943.

Napoleone Moriani died March 4, 1878.

First performance of Tchaikowsky's ballet "Swan Lake" was
given on March 4, 1877, in Moscow.

Edoardo Mascheroni died March 4, 1941.

March Fifth

> Without haste, without rest. This should be the motto
> of every aspirant for musical honors. --Goethe

Edward MacDowell's Piano Concerto No. 2 in D minor was
first performed on March 5, 1889, in New York City.

Heitor Villa-Lobos was born March 5, 1887.

World premiere of "Mefistofele" was presented at La Scala
in Milan on March 5, 1868.

Ezio Pinza sang a last Don Giovanni at the Metropolitan Opera on March 5, 1948.

Alfredo Casella died March 5, 1947.

Thomas Arne died March 5, 1778.

Arthur W. Foote was born March 5, 1853.

Lorin Maazel was born March 5, 1930.

March Sixth

> The crucial test of good vocal music is the intrinsic
> merit of the music when separated from the words,
> and that merit consists in the beauty of musical
> thought. --Hiller

Premiere performance of Bellini's "La Sonnambula" took
place at the Teatro Carcano, Milan, on March 6, 1831, with
Giuditta Pasta and Giovanni-Battista Rubini. The opera was
dedicated "al celebre Francesco Pollini," an esteemed composer of the day.

World premiere of Verdi's "La Traviata" was given March
6, 1853, at the Teatro la Fenice in Venice. The first Violetta was Fanny Salvini-Donatelli.

Marietta Alboni, one of the greatest of contraltos and Rossini's only pupil, was born March 6, 1823.

Rubin Goldmark died March 6, 1936.

Metropolitan premiere of "Le Coq d'Or" was given on March
6, 1918.

John Philip Sousa died March 6, 1932.

Zoltan Kodaly died March 6, 1967.

Nelson Eddy, baritone of concert, radio and screen, died
March 6, 1967.

Friedrich Bechstein died March 6, 1900.

March Seventh

> Music should strike fire from the heart of man, and
> bring tears from the eyes of woman. --Beethoven

Maurice Ravel was born March 7, 1875.

Operatic debut of Jenny Lind in Weber's "Der Freischutz"
took place on March 7, 1838, in Stockholm.

Johannes Brahms attended his last concert on March 7, 1897,
when Hans Richter directed a performance of his Fourth

Symphony.

Metropolitan premiere of "Andrea Chenier" was presented on March 7, 1920, with Beniamino Gigli in the title role and, as Madeleine, Claudio Muzio, who was superbly cast.

March Eighth

> The mind alone, whose every thought is rhythm, can embody music, can comprehend its mysteries, its divine inspirations, and can speak to the senses of its intellectual revelation. --Beethoven

Sir Thomas Beecham died March 8, 1961.

Giovanni Martinelli sang a last Pollione in "Norma" at the Metropolitan Opera March 8, 1945.

Hector Berlioz died March 8, 1869.

Carl Philipp Emanuel Bach was born March 8, 1714.

Ruggiero Leoncavallo was born March 8, 1858.

Paul Juon was born March 8, 1872.

Alan Hovhaness was born March 8, 1911.

Adolphe Nourrit died March 8, 1839.

March Ninth

> When any master holds
> Twixt chin and hand a violin of mine,
> He will be glad that Stradivari lived,
> Made violins and made them of the best. --
> George Eliot's "Stradivarius"

Franz Liszt heard Paganini for the first time and sketched the transcription of his Campanella Studies on March 9, 1831.

World premiere of Verdi's opera 'Nabucco" was given on March 9, 1842, at La Scala in Milan with Giuseppini Strepponi in the cast.

Stradivarius--
from a painting by E.J.C. Hamman.

Samuel Barber was born March 9, 1910.

Verdi's "Ernani" was heard for the first time on March 9, 1844, in Venice with the Vienna trained soprano, Sophie Lowe.

Thomas Schippers was born March 9, 1930.

March Tenth

> Of the nine the loveliest three
>   Are painting, music, poetry.
> But thou are freest of the free
>   Matchless muse of harmony. --Grillparzer
> (Translated by Sir Walter Scott for Moschele's album
> in 1828)

Ignaz Moscheles died March 10, 1870.

Mozart played the first performance of his Concerto in C Major on March 10, 1785, at the Burgtheater in Vienna.

Operatic tenor Napoleone Moriani was born March 10, 1808.

Muzio Clementi died March 10, 1832.

Metropolitan premiere of "La Rondine" took place March 10, 1928. Vincenzo Bellezza conducted and the cast included Lucrezia Bori and Beniamino Gigli.

Arthur Honegger was born March 10, 1892.

March Eleventh

> The first and most indispensable quality of any artist
> is to feel respect for great men, and to bow down in
> spirit before them; to recognize their merits, and not
> to endeavor to extinguish their great flame in order
> that his own feeble rushlight may burn a little brighter.
> --Mendelssohn

Mendelssohn presented J. S. Bach's "Passion According to St. Matthew" in Berlin on March 11, 1829, and thus initiated the Bach revival.

World premiere performance of Verdi's "Rigoletto" was presented at the Teatro la Fenice in Venice on March 11, 1851. Felice Varesi created the role of Rigoletto.

Bellini's opera "I Capuleti ed Montecchi" was first performed March 11, 1830, with Giulia Grisi and Maria Caradori-Allan.

Ernestine Schumann-Heink's last Metropolitan appearance (at age of 70) was on March 11, 1932.

Geraldine Farrar died March 11, 1967.

World premiere of Verdi's "Don Carlos" was produced in Paris on March 11, 1867. The two leading stars of the cast were Marie-Constance Sasse and Jean-Baptiste Faure.

Henry Cowell was born March 11, 1897.

March Twelfth

> Christianity is the only soil in which music could grow
> and develop herself with a splendor never conceived by
> the ancients. --Ernst Pauer

John Bull died March 12, 1628.

Thomas Arne was born March 12, 1710.

Verdi's opera "Simon Boccanegra" was first performed
March 12, 1857, in Venice.

Harold Bauer died March 12, 1951.

Friedrich Kuhlau died March 12, 1832.

Hans Knappertsbusch was born March 12, 1888.

March Thirteenth

> Healthy criticism, such as is based on true art-knowl-
> edge, is very healthful to the progress of art; yes, we
> may call it the very life of art. --Merz

Hugo Wolf, music critic of the "Salonblott," was born March
13, 1860.

Mendelssohn's Violin Concerto in E minor, a favorite of all,
was first performed at the Gwendhaus, Leipzig on March 13,
1845, with Ferdinand David as soloist and Mendelssohn conducting.

Emma Eames made her world debut as Juliette at the Opera
in Paris on March 13, 1889. It was Gounod himself who
selected her to sing in his opera.

Maestro Fritz Busch was born March 13, 1890.

Enrico Tamberlik died March 13, 1889.

It was at the Cologne Opera that Bruno Walter made his conducting debut on March 13, 1894, directing Albert Lortzing's
comic opera 'Der Waffenschmied."

Maria Müller died in Bayreuth March 13, 1958.

Felice Varesi died March 13, 1889.

March Fourteenth

> Sacrifice all the trivialities of social life to thy art. --
> The Odyssey

World premiere of Verdi's "Macbeth" took place in Florence on March 14, 1847, with Felice Varesi as Macbeth.

Johann Strauss (the Elder) was born March 14, 1804.

Sullivan's "The Mikado" was first produced on March 14, 1885, in London.

Georg Philipp Telemann was born March 14, 1681.

Feodor Chaliapin sang a last Boris Godunov on March 14, 1929, at the Metropolitan Opera.

March Fifteenth

> He is a good musician who understands the music without the score, and the score without the music. --
> Schumann

Koussevitzky gave the world premier of Scriabin's last symphony, "Prometheus," on March 15, 1911.

Maria Luigi Cherubini died March 15, 1842.

Kurt Baum was born March 15, 1908.

First performance of Ravel's "Rhapsodie espagnole" was given March 15, 1908, in Paris.

March Sixteenth

> Melody is, and ever will be, the very flower of music.
> --Ambros

World premiere of Bellini's "Beatrice di Tenda" was presented March 16, 1833, at the Teatro La Fenice. The cast included Giuditta Pasta and Alberico Curioni.

Massenet's opera "Thais" was first heard on March 16, 1894, in Paris. Sybil Sanderson, Jean-Francois Delmas and Albert Alvarez sang in the world premiere.

Metropolitan debut of Irene Dalis, portraying Princess Eboli in Verdi's "Don Carlos," took place March 16, 1957.

Giovanni Pergolesi died March 16, 1736.

Teresa Berganza was born March 16, 1934.

March Seventeenth

> The value of the sketches made by Chopin's extremely delicate pencil has not yet been acknowledged and emphasized sufficiently. It has become customary in our days to regard as great composers only those who have written at least half a dozen operas, as many oratorios, and several symphonies. --Franz Liszt

Frederic Chopin's Second Piano Concerto in E Minor was first heard at Chopin's concert debut in Warsaw on March 17, 1830.

Manuel Patricio Garcia was born March 17, 1805.

Premiere of Marvin David Levy's "Mourning Becomes Elektra" was presented on March 17, 1967.

Robert Goldsand was born March 17, 1911.

Jacques Halevy died March 17, 1862.

Dinu Lipatti was born March 17, 1917.

March Eighteenth

> A theme! a theme! great nature! give a theme;
> Let me begin my dream. --Keats

Nicolai Rimsky-Korsakov was born March 18, 1844.

Willem van Hoogstraten was born March 18, 1884.

John Kirkpatrick was born March 18, 1905.

Francesco Malipiero was born March 18, 1882.

World premiere of Rachmaninoff's Piano Concerto No. 4 was presented March 18, 1927, in Philadelphia, with the composer as guest artist and Leopold Stokowski conducting.

March Nineteenth

> Every one who thinks genius can be without understanding, thinks without understanding himself. --Jean Paul Richter

First performance of Gounod's "Faust" was presented at the Theatre-Lyrique, Paris, on March 19, 1859.

World premiere of Tchaikowsky's Nutcracker Suite took place on March 19, 1892, in St. Petersburg.

The notable modern revival of Handel's "Alcina" began in England on March 19, 1957, when the Handel Opera Society presented Joan Sutherland in the title role.

American premiere of "Boris Godunov" was given at the Metropolitan Opera, March 19, 1913 with Toscanini conducting. The cast included Adamo Didur, Louise Homer and Leon Rothier.

Max Reger was born March 19, 1873.

American premiere of "Wozzeck" took place on March 19, 1931, with Leopold Stokowski conducting.

Ludwig Wullner died March 19, 1938.

March Twentieth

> Just as a writer who speaks to the heart is sure to please, so is a composer who gives the player something which he cannot only play and enjoy himself, but make others enjoy too. --Zelter

Sviatoslav Richter was born March 20, 1914.

Beniamino Gigli, greatest of the post-Caruso tenors, was born March 20, 1890.

Lauritz Melchior was born March 20, 1890.

Johann Ludwig Dussek died March 20, 1812.

New York Symphony Society united with the New York Phil-harmonic Society on March 20, 1928, forming the Philhar-monic-Symphony Society Orchestra of New York.

March Twenty-first

> To me it is with Bach as if the eternal harmonies dis-coursed with one another. --Goethe

Johann Sebastian Bach was born March 21, 1685.

Johann Sebastian Bach,
born March 21, 1685.

. Metropolitan premiere of Meyerbeer's "Le Prophete" occurred during the first season on March 21, 1884.   Augusto
Vianesi conducted.

Modest Moussorgsky was born March 21, 1839.

First Metropolitan performance of "Pelleas et Melisande"
was presented on March 21, 1925, with Lucrezia Bori and
Edward Johnson.

Alexander Glazunov died March 21, 1936.

Robert Goldsand made his American debut with a recital at
Carnegie Hall on March 21, 1927.

Metropolitan debut of Cornell MacNeil took place March 21,
1959.

Willem Mengelberg died March 21, 1951.

Adolf Brodsky was born March 21, 1851.

March Twenty-second

> Musical art recognizes two kinds of music--artistic
> music, the production of the artist, and national music,
> the production of the people. If we liken music to flow-
> ers the former would be the cultivated, the latter the
> wild flowers.--Christiani

Jean Baptiste Lully died March 22, 1687.

Schubert's Symphony in C Major was first performed March
22, 1839, in Leipzig.

March Twenty-third

> A deeper insight into Bach's works cannot fail to further
> the progress of art.--Moscheles

First performance of J. S. Bach's "Passion According to St.
Matthew" was heard on March 23, 1729, in Leipzig.

Haydn's Surprise Symphony was presented for the first time
March 23, 1792, in London.

Egon Petri was born March 23, 1881.

Caroline Unger died March 23, 1877.

The first performance of "Aphrodite" was given on March 23, 1906, at the Opera Comique in Paris with the American singer Mary Garden.

March Twenty-fourth

> Work alone praises or condemns its masters, and I therefore measure every one by that standard. --Johann Sebastian Bach

J. S. Bach completed the sixth Brandenburg Concerto on March 24, 1721.

Maria Felicia Malibran was born March 24, 1808.

American premiere of "Cosi Fan Tutti" was presented at the Metropolitan Opera, March 24, 1922, with Florence Easton, Lucrezia Bori, Giuseppe De Luca and Adamo Didur.

American debut of Francesco Tamagno in Verdi's "Otello" took place on March 24, 1890, at the Metropolitan Opera.

Enrique Granados died March 24, 1916.

Byron Janis was born March 24, 1928.

Mathilda Marchesi, famous vocal teacher, was born March 24, 1821.

Gino Marinuzzi was born March 24, 1882.

March Twenty-fifth

> 'Canta Canta' (sing, sing), coaxed and shouted Toscanini to his instrumentalists and singers; he wanted at all costs smooth-flowing legato tone all the time. Look at the results he secured!

Arturo Toscanini was born March 25, 1867.

Claude DeBussy died March 25, 1918.

The Metropolitan Opera presented their first German Meistersinger, March 25, 1901, with Jean De Reszke, Edouard
De Reszke, Johanna Gadski and Ernestine Schumann-Heink.

Bela Bartok was born March 25, 1881.

March Twenty-sixth

> In Beethoven imagination, feeling, intellect, and charac-
> ter are developed with equal power, and in perfect har-
> mony with one another. --Von Elterlein

Ludwig van Beethoven died March 26, 1827.

Wilhelm Backhaus was born March 26, 1884.

Franz Schubert gave his only public concert on March 26,
1828, in Vienna.

Pierre Boulez, French avant-garde composer and conductor,
was born March 26, 1925.

Bernhardt Breitkopf died March 26, 1777.

Andre Cluytens was born March 26, 1905.

American premiere performance of Schumann's Piano Concerto in A Minor was presented March 26, 1859.

March Twenty-seventh

> I require no undercurrent of thought when I hear music,
> which is not to me 'a mere medium to elevate the mind
> to piety, ' as they say here, but a distinct language
> speaking plainly to me; for though the sense is expressed
> by the words, it is equally contained in the music. This
> is the case with the 'Passion' of Sebastian Bach. --
> Mendelssohn, extract of a letter to Zelter from Rome
> in 1831.

First performance of the "Passion According to St. John" by
Johann Sebastian Bach was given on March 27, 1723, in
Leipzig.

Ralph Vaughan-Williams' "A London Symphony" was first performed March 27, 1914, at the Queens Hall, London, with Geoffrey Toye conducting.

World premiere of "La Rondine" took place on March 27, 1917, in Monte Carlo.

Vincent D'Indy was born March 27, 1851.

Genevieve Ward was born March 27, 1833.

March Twenty-eighth

Among the many essential qualifications of the musician the grandest of all is a poetic imagination. It reveals to him many beautiful things that elude the casual observer. --Lovejoy

Modest Moussorgsky died March 28, 1881.

Sergei Rachmaninoff died March 28, 1943.

World premiere of "Andrea Chenier" took place at La Scala, Milan, on March 28, 1896.

Maestro Anton Seidl died March 28, 1898.

Rudolph Serkin was born March 28, 1903.

Rosina Lhevinne was born March 28, 1880.

Maestro Willem Mengelberg was born March 28, 1871.

Antonio Tamburini was born March 28, 1800.

It was Easter Monday, March 28, 1842, that the Vienna Court Orchestra played its first performance as a concert ensemble. The founder was Otto Nicolai, Court Opera conductor and composer of "The Merry Wives of Windsor."

March Twenty-ninth

He (Beethoven) was like a Titan wrestling with the Gods. --Wagner

Beethoven's first public appearance as virtuoso and composer was on March 29, 1795, at a Vienna concert.

Tchaikowsky's "Eugene Onegin" was first performed March 29, 1879, in Moscow.

E. Power Biggs was born March 29, 1906.

Lucrezia Bori gave her farewell program March 29, 1936, at the Metropolitan Opera.

William Walton was born March 29, 1902.

Johann Andreas Amon died March 29, 1825.

March Thirtieth

> Beneath their flowers I dream, a silent chord. I can not wake my own strings to music; but under the hands of those who comprehend me, I become an eloquent friend. Wanderer, ere thou goest, try me! The more trouble thou takest with me, the more lovely will be the tones with which I shall reward thee. --Schumann

Julliard Musical Foundation was incorporated on March 30, 1920.

Milko Kelemen was born March 30, 1924.

Frederic Austin was born March 30, 1872.

March Thirty-first

> Joseph Haydn! A man who always held his gifts as a trust from the Maker of all, and who recognized his own stewardship by inscribing most of his writings, 'To the praise of God.' --Ernst Pauer

Franz Joseph Haydn was born March 31, 1732.

The Spring Symphony No. 1 of Robert Schumann's was first heard March 31, 1841, in Leipzig.

Domenico Donzelli, celebrated tenor during the 1834-1840 period, died March 31, 1873.

Clemens Heinrich Krauss was born March 31, 1892.

Elley Ney died March 31, 1968.

APRIL

Music is the essence of order,
and leads to all that is good,
just and beautiful. --Plato

April First

No kind of pianoforte music contains so much that is so excellent as the study, the etude. The reasons are simple: its form is one of the easiest and most attractive, and its aim is so clear and firmly fixed that it is impossible to fail in it. --Schumann

Serge Rachmaninoff was born April 1, 1873.

Ferruccio Busoni was born April 1, 1866.

Premiere of Menotti's opera "Amelia Goes to the Ball" took place in Philadelphia on April 1, 1937.

Kirsten Flagstad sang a last Alceste on April 1, 1952, at the Metropolitan Opera House.

April Second

I willingly renounce the world, which has no presentiment that music is a higher revelation than all their wisdom and philosophy. --Beethoven

Premiere performance of Beethoven's First Symphony took place at the National Court Theatre in Vienna on April 2, 1800. The conductor was Paul Wranitzky.

Operatic debut of Lauritz Melchior took place April 2, 1913.

Kurt Herbert Adler was born April 2, 1905.

Simon Barere died in New York City while playing in Carnegie Hall on April 2, 1951.

Wallingford Riegger died April 2, 1961.

April Third

> Good music has a logic of its own; none more severe,
> and surely none so fascinating; for it leads, it charms
> into the Infinite. --Dwight

The Seventh Symphony of Sibelius was first played in America on April 3, 1926, Leopold Stokowski conducting.

Johannes Brahms died April 3, 1897.

The Leipzig Conservatory opened officially under Mendelssohn's direction on April 3, 1843.

The first issue of the "Neue Zeitschrift fur Musik" was published in Leipzig on April 3, 1834, by Robert Schumann,
Friedrich Wieck and others.

Maestro Sixten Ehrling was born April 3, 1918.

Jean De Reszke died April 3, 1925.

Frances Alda was married April 3, 1910 to Gatti-Casazza,
director of the Metropolitan Opera House.

The London Symphony gave the U.S. premiere of Richard
Rodney Bennett's "Variations for Orchestra" on April 3,
1966, in New York.

Kurt Weill died April 3, 1950.

April Fourth

> Seek among your associates those who know more than
> you. --Schumann

Hans Richter was born April 4, 1843.

"The Moldau" of Smetana's was first performed April 4,
1874.

Pierre Monteux was born April 4, 1875.

World premiere of Meyerbeer's "Le Pardon de Ploermel"
was presented at the Opera Comique, Paris, on April 4,

1859. The opera was an immediate success.

Toscanini conducted his last concert with the NBC Symphony in Carnegie Hall on April 4, 1954, just after his 87th birthday.

George Whitefield Chadwick died April 4, 1931.

April Fifth

> Even in the most intricate compositions, and particularly in those which express his most mysterious feelings, the artist should employ simple form in order to render his ideas clear and intelligible. --Stephen Heller

The Second Symphony of Beethoven was first performed April 5, 1803. At the same concert, his Piano Concerto No. 3 was introduced with the composer playing the solo part.

Ludwig Spohr was born April 5, 1784.

Strauss' "Die Fledermaus" was first heard on April 5, 1874, in Vienna.

Mary Costa was born April 5, 1930.

Premiere of Stravinsky's "Rite of Spring" was given April 5, 1914, in Paris.

Herbert von Karajan was born April 5, 1908.

Albert Roussel was born April 5, 1869.

Premiere performance of Alexander Goehr's "Arden muss Sterben" took place on April 5, 1967, at the Hamburg Opera.

Sebastien Erard, founder of a famous firm of piano and harp manufacturers, was born April 5, 1752.

April Sixth

> O Music, thou who bringest the receding waves of eternity nearer to the weary heart of man as he stands upon the shore and longs to cross over, art thou the evening

breeze of life or the morning air of the future?--Jean
Paul Richter

George Frederic Handel conducted "The Messiah" at Covent
Garden, London, on April 6, 1759.

Beethoven's "Missa Solemnis" was first performed at St.
Petersburg on April 6, 1824.

Johann Kuhnau was born April 6, 1660.

The Royal Italian Opera, Covent Garden, London, was inaugurated on April 6, 1847.

Arabella Goddard died April 6, 1922.

Premiere of Miklos Rozsa's Piano Concerto took place April
6, 1967, featuring Leonard Pennario as soloist with the Los
Angeles Philharmonic.

April Seventh

The language of tones belongs equally to all mankind,
and melody is the absolute language in which the musician speaks to every heart.--Wagner

First public performance of the famous "Eroica" by Ludwig
van Beethoven was given on April 7, 1805, in Vienna, with
the composer conducting.

Giovanni-Battista Rubini, greatest of the early nineteenth-
century virtuoso tenors, was born April 7, 1795.

Robert Casadesus was born April 7, 1899.

American premiere of "Robert le Diable," opera by Meyerbeer, was given on April 7, 1834, in New York.

April Eighth

The pleasure which the work of a musician affords you
is his very life-blood; the trouble it has cost him you
do not know. He gives you his very best: the essence
of his life, the outflow of his genius, and yet you grudge
him a simple wreath of flowers.--Schumann

Gaetano Donizetti died April 8, 1848.

Franco Corelli was born April 8, 1923.

Maestro Josef Krips was born April 8, 1902.

Sir Adrian Boult was born April 8, 1889.

Claudio Merulo, first of the great organ virtuosi, was born April 8, 1533.

Giuseppina Grassini of La Scala fame was born on April 8, 1773. Kings and princes fell for her. Napoleon, captivated by her beauty and artistry, coaxed her to Paris.

Giuseppe Tartini was born April 8, 1692.

Ponchielli's "La Gioconda" began triumphantly at La Scala, Milan, on April 8, 1876, with Gayarre in the role of Enza.

Charles T. Griffes died April 8, 1920.

Janis Martin made her La Scala debut on April 8, 1967, as Venus, under the baton of Wolfgang Sawallisch.

Anton Diabelli died April 8, 1858.

Arthur W. Foote died April 8, 1937.

April Ninth

> A certain music never known before
> Here lulled the pensive, melancholy mind. --Thomson

Giuditta Pasta, for whom Bellini wrote "Norma," was born April 9, 1798.

Joseph Fischer was born April 9, 1841.

Efrem Zimbalist was born April 9, 1889.

Maestro Antal Dorati was born April 9, 1906.

Sir Paola Tosti was born April 9, 1846.

First performance in America of Shostakovitch's Fifth Symphony was given on April 9, 1938.

April Tenth

> We must ever strive after the highest, and never weary
> because others have earlier obtained the good to which
> we aspire.--Mendelssohn

Eugene d'Albert was born April 10, 1864.

Brahms' "Deutsches Requiem" was first performed April 10,
1868, at Bremen.

Victor de Sabata was born April 10, 1892.

World premiere of Montemezzi's "L'Amore dei Tre Re" was
presented on April 10, 1913, at La Scala with Tullio Serafin
conducting.

Herbert Graf was born April 10, 1904.

April Eleventh

> It is an indisputable fact that in the union of poetry and
> music the stronger and more immediate effect is pro-
> duced by the latter.--Ferdinand Hiller

First concert of the New Symphony Orchestra, dedicated to
modern music, took place in New York City on April 11,
1919, with Edgard Varese conducting.

Inauguration of the Concertgebouw in Amsterdam was on
April 11, 1888.

Eric Blom died April 11, 1959.

"An evening with Meyerbeer" was held by Friends of French
Opera on April 11, 1967, at Carnegie Hall.

Beverly Sills made her debut at La Scala on April 11, 1969,
singing Palmira in Rossini's "Seige of Corinth."

April Twelfth

> Sighing I turned away; but ere
> Night fell I heard, or seemed to hear
> Music that sorrow comes not near
>   A ritual hymn,
> Chaunted in love that casts out fear
> By Seraphim. --
>
> Wordsworth

Lily Pons was born April 12, 1904.

Premiere of Weber's opera "Oberon" took place on April 12, 1826, with the composer conducting at Covent Garden, London. It was his last triumph.

Maestro Giorgio Polacco was born April 12, 1875.

Caffarelli, virtuoso master of song for whom Handel wrote the famous "Largo" from "Xerxes," was born April 12, 1710.

Franz Kullak was born April 12, 1844.

Joseph Lanner was born April 12, 1801.

Feodor Chaliapin died April 12, 1938.

April Thirteenth

> To him I bend the knees.   For Handel is the greatest, ablest composer that ever lived. --Beethoven

Handel's oratorio "The Messiah" was first performed April 13, 1742, in Dublin.   The audience, with George II at its head, rose at the Hallelujah Chorus, and the custom survives to the present day.

Van Cliburn won the International Tchaikowsky Competition in Moscow on April 13, 1958.

It was Friday, the 13th of April in 1900, that Mary Garden had her chance to finish the performance of "Louise" at the Opera Comique in Paris when the prima donna fell ill.   She played the part so beautifully that for the next 200 productions no one else was permitted to sing it.

Mario Castelnuovo-Tedesco was born April 13, 1895.

Ethel Leginska was born April 13, 1886.

Felicien David was born April 13, 1810.

Ludwig Rellstab was born April 13, 1799.

American Guild of Organists was founded on April 13, 1896.

Nino Sanzogno was born April 13, 1911.

April Fourteenth

> Learn all there is to learn, and then choose your own
> path. --Handel

George Frederic Handel died April 14, 1759.

World premiere of "Lakme" by Delibes was presented on
April 14, 1883, in Paris. Marie Van Zandt, for whom Delibes composed the music, had the title role.

On April 14, 1957, "Anna Bolena" was triumphantly revived
at La Scala, Milan, with Maria Callas in the title role.
The conductor was Gianandrea Gavazzeni. Many critics
thought it Callas' greatest role.

Joseph Lanner died April 14, 1843.

Salvatore Baccaloni was born April 14, 1900.

Eduard van Beinum died April 14, 1959.

Anton Rubinstein made his Paris debut as a pianist on April
14, 1857.

April Fifteenth

> Thus did Jubal to his race reveal
> Music, their larger soul,
>   where woe and weal,
> Filling the resonant chords,

> the song, the dance,
> Moved with a wider-winged utterance. --
>
> George Eliot

Symphony No. 2 of Beethoven, dedicated to Prince Karl Lichnowsky, was first performed on April 15, 1803, in Vienna.

Operatic debut of Frances Alda took place on April 15, 1904, at the Opera Comique in Paris.

Yury Arbatsky was born April 15, 1911.

World premiere of "The Pageant of P. T. Barnum" by Douglas Moore was given April 15, 1926, in Cleveland, Ohio.

April Sixteenth

> An artist will be more or less inspired according to how his thoughts correspond and awaken in him his own sensitiveness. --La Vallee

Handel's opera "Alcina" was first performed on April 16, 1735, in Covent Garden, London.

Johann Baptist Cramer died April 16, 1858.

World premiere of "Le Prophete" by Meyerbeer was given April 16, 1849, in Paris. The role of Fides was created by Pauline Viardot-Garcia.

Alice Ehlers was born April 16, 1890.

First American performance of Verdi's "Otello" was presented April 16, 1888, in New York.

April Seventeenth

> The notes I handle no better than many pianists. But the pauses between the notes--ah, that is where the art resides. --Artur Schnabel

Artur Schnabel was born April 17, 1882.

Gilbert-Louis Duprez made his debut as Arnold in Rossini's

"William Tell" on April 17, 1837.

Louis Biancolli was born April 17, 1907.

First performance in America of "Die Zauberflote" (The Magic Flute) by Mozart was given April 17, 1833, in New York.

Alfred Hertz died April 17, 1942.

April Eighteenth

> Although instrumental music cannot be sung, yet the player may render by adequate modulation its meaning, and the sad or joyous thoughts it is intended to express.
> --Praetorius

Leopold Stokowski was born April 18, 1882.

Cecile Chaminade died April 18, 1944.

Frida Leider was born April 18, 1888.

Ottorino Respighi died April 18, 1936.

Franz von Suppe was born April 18, 1819.

April Nineteenth

> Simplicity, truth and nature are the great touchstones of the beautiful in all artistic creation. --Gluck

First performance of Gluck's "Iphigenie en Aulide" was presented on April 19, 1774, in Paris.

Karl W. Gehrkens, American musical editor and educator, was born April 19, 1882.

Barbara Marchisio died April 19, 1919.

April Twentieth

> Art is a great fugue into which the different individualities and nationalities step and become resolved, like the

different subjects, one after another. --<u>Schumann</u>

Henry C. Colles was born April 20, 1879.

Gregor Piatigorsky was born April 20, 1903.

Nicolas Miaskovsky was born April 20, 1881.

Johann Christoph Denner died April 20, 1707.

April Twenty-first

Uninterrupted harmony would soon become as fatiguing
as a constant sunshine. Harmony after discord is a
new pleasure; sunshine after rain gives new enjoyment.
--<u>Christiani</u>

First performance of Prokofieff's Classical Symphony in D
Major took place on April 21, 1918, in Leningrad, with the
composer conducting.

Leonard Warren was born April 21, 1911.

On April 21, 1873, the noted French baritone, Victor Maurel,
made his London debut at Covent Garden as Renato in "Un
Ballo in Maschero."

Randall Thompson was born April 21, 1899.

April Twenty-second

I am what I am because I was industrious; whoever is
equally sedulous will be equally successful. --<u>J. Sebastian
Bach</u>

J. S. Bach was elected Cantor of St. Thomas in Leipzig on
April 22, 1723.

Yehudi Menuhin was born April 22, 1916.

Paris first heard "Aida" on April 22, 1876, at the Theatre
Italien, with Teresa Stolz and Edouard de Reszke, the latter
making his operatic debut.

Geraldine Farrar sang her final operatic role at the Metro-

politan Opera on April 22, 1922, when she appeared in "Zaza."
Edouard Lalo died April 22, 1892.

April Twenty-third

> Music is never stationary; successive forms and styles
> are only like so many resting places--like tents pitched
> and taken down again on the road to the Ideal.--Franz
> Liszt

Serge Prokofieff was born April 23, 1891.

Olive Fremstad gave her farewell performance at the Metropolitan Opera on April 23, 1914.

Elisabeth Schumann died April 23, 1952.

First performance of Alfred Casella's rhapsody, "Italia,"
was presented in Paris on April 23, 1910, under the direction of the composer.

April Twenty-fourth

> Music, oh how faint, how weak,
>   Language fades before thy spell!
> Why should Feeling ever speak,
>   When thou canst breathe her soul so well!
> Friendship's balmy words may feign,
>   Love's are ev'n more false than they;
> Oh! 'tis only music's strain
>   Can sweetly soothe and not betray.--
>
>   Moore

Padre Martini was born April 24, 1706.

Johann Philipp Kirnberger was born April 24, 1721.

Haydn's "Die Jahreszeiten" was first performed April 24,
1801, in Vienna.

Girolama Crescentini died April 24, 1846.

April Twenty-fifth

> Great is song used to great ends. --<u>Tennyson</u>

Pauline Lucca was born April 25, 1841.

Puccini's "Turandot" was first performed April 25, 1926, at La Scala, Milan, with Toscanini conducting. Leading roles were sung by Rosa Raisa and Miguel Fleta.

Astrid Varnay was born April 25, 1918.

Jerdy Fitelberg died April 25, 1951.

April Twenty-sixth

> Music is one of the greatest educators in the world, and the study of it in its highest departments, such as com- position, harmony, and counterpoint, develops the mind as much as the study of mathematics or the languages. --<u>Anon</u>.

Handel's "Serse" (in which occurs the famous Largo) was first produced on April 26, 1738, in London.

Baron von Flotow was born April 26, 1812.

Symphony No. 1 of Jean Sibelius was first performed April 26, 1899, in Helsingfors.

April Twenty-seventh

> He who would do a great thing well must first have done the simplest thing perfectly. --<u>Cady</u>

Igor Oistrakh, son of David Oistrakh, was born April 27, 1931.

Alexander Scriabin died April 27, 1915.

"Romeo and Juliet" (Gounod) was first performed at the Thea- tre-Lyrique in Paris on April 27, 1867. Marie Miolan- Carvalho was the heroine of the world premiere.

Sigismund Thalberg died April 27, 1871.

April Twenty-eighth

But few artists approach the perfection which is needed in unadorned form or simple tune.--<u>Christiani</u>

European debut of Glen Gould was in Berlin with the Berlin Philharmonic on April 28, 1957.

Harold Bauer was born April 28, 1873.

World premiere of Meyerbeer's last opera "L'Africane" was presented on April 28, 1865, in Paris.

Luisa Tetrazzini died April 28, 1940.

Emil Von Sauer died April 28, 1942.

April Twenty-ninth

The elements of orchestration are those of painting. The composition <u>per se</u> represents the design; the melody the outline; harmony the light and shade; and instrumentation the coloring.--<u>J. Raff</u>

Sir Thomas Beecham was born April 29, 1879.

Sir Malcolm Sargent was born April 29, 1895.

Wallingford Riegger was born April 29, 1885.

Haydn's "Die Schopfung" was first performed on April 29, 1798, in Vienna.

Jean de Reszke sang a last Lohengrin at the Metropolitan Opera on April 29, 1901.

April Thirtieth

To believe that one can judge a work of art by first impressions is one of the strangest and most dangerous of delusions.--<u>Claude Debussy</u>

"Pelleas and Melisande" was first performed at the Opera Comique in Paris on April 30, 1902, with Mary Garden and Jean Perier in the title roles.

Franz Lehar was born April 30, 1870.

Louise Homer was born April 30, 1871.

Robert Shaw was born April 30, 1916.

Giorgio Polacco died April 30, 1960.

MAY

How divine is the vocation of art! --<u>Mendelssohn</u>

May First

I tell you before God and on my word as an honest man
that your son is the greatest composer I have ever
heard of. --<u>Josef Haydn to Leopold Mozart</u>

"Le Nozze di Figaro" was first performed on May 1, 1786
at the Burgtheater in Vienna.

Antonin Dvorak died May 1, 1904.

World premiere of Cesar Franck's Symphonic Variations for
Piano and Orchestra was given on May 1, 1885.

Walter Susskind was born May 1, 1913.

First American performance of "Semiramide" was given May
1, 1837, in New Orleans.

May Second

Counterpoint is related to mathematics. A fool with
patience becomes a respectable savant in that, but for
the part of genius, melody, it has no rules. --
<u>De Stendhal</u>

Alessandro Scarlatti was born May 2, 1660.

Giacomo Meyerbeer died May 2, 1864.

On May 2, 1966, David Diamond's Piano Concerto and Fifth
Symphony were given their premiere performance by the
New York Philharmonic under the direction of Leonard Bern-
stein.

Michael Rabin was born May 2, 1936.

World premiere of Prokofiev's "Peter and the Wolf" was presented in Moscow on May 2, 1936.

First performance of Bruckner's "Te Deum" was given in Vienna on May 2, 1885.

May Third

> When an artist has been able to say, 'I came, I saw, I conquered,' it has been at the end of patient practice.
> --George Eliot

Marcel Dupre was born May 3, 1886.

Evelyn Lear gave her first New York recital on May 3, 1967, at Philharmonic Hall.

Fanny Persiani died May 3, 1867.

William Beale died May 3, 1854.

Franz Von Biber died May 3, 1704.

Virgil Fox was born May 3, 1912.

Max Alvary was born May 3, 1856.

May Fourth

> Whoever knows me knows that I owe much to Sebastian Bach, that I have studied him thoroughly and well, and that I acknowledge him only as my model. --Haydn

Haydn's London Symphony in D Major was first produced in London on May 4, 1795.

Bartolommeo Cristofori, Italian harpsichord maker who is credited with the invention of the piano, was born May 4, 1655.

Roberta Peters was born May 4, 1930.

It was on May 4, 1848, that Chopin heard Jenny Lind's

"Amina" and he wrote to his friend, Grzymala: "Her singing is infallibly pure and true and above all, I admire her
piano passages, the charm of which is indescribable."

May 4, 1904, was declared a National Day of Mourning for
Antonin Dvorak in Prague.

George Enesco died May 4, 1955.

Camille Pleyel died May 4, 1855.

Claudio Merulo died May 4, 1604.

May Fifth

> To commune with God is man's greatest privilege and
> duty. We may address the Deity through the medium
> of music, as well as through words, since in music
> we may express our most secret feelings. --Merz

Handel's opera "Alessandra" opened on May 5, 1726.

Hans Pfitzner was born May 5, 1869.

DeBussy appeared in public for the last time as pianist on
May 5, 1917, playing his Sonata for piano and violin with
Gaston Poulet in Paris.

Inauguration of Carnegie Hall in New York took place on
May 5, 1891.   P. I. Tchaikowsky was guest conductor.

Frank La Forge died May 5, 1953.

May Sixth

> As Beethoven regarded his art as something sacred,
> which he placed higher than all philosophy, so has a
> refined artist an innate horror of all vulgar, frivolous
> and effeminate music. --Ambros

Heinrich Ernst was born May 6, 1814.

Hans Jelmoli died May 6, 1936.

Anton Raaf, German singer and friend of Mozart, was born

May 6, 1714.

American debut in New York of Leopold Damrosch as violinist, composer, and conductor took place on May 6, 1871.

Louise Homer died May 6, 1947.

May Seventh

> In order to please everybody at once it is necessary to compromise and in questions of art he who compromises is sure to disappear in a short time. --Richard Wagner

Johannes Brahms was born May 7, 1833.

Peter Ilyich Tchaikowsky was born May 7, 1840.

Peter Ilyich Tchaikowsky,
born May 7, 1840.

On May 7, 1824, in Vienna, Beethoven appeared on a public concert platform for the last time. The occasion was the premiere of his last symphony--the Ninth.

Maestro Anton Seidl was born May 7, 1850.

Felix von Weingartner died May 7, 1942.

Oscar Hammerstein was born May 7, 1848.

Euphrosyne Parepa-Rosa was born May 7, 1830.

May Eighth

> The study of the history of music, and the hearing of
> masterworks of different epochs, will cure one of vanity
> and self-adulation. --Robert Schumann

Giovanni Paisiello was born May 8, 1740.

Louis M. Gottschalk was born May 8, 1829.

William Sydeman was born May 8, 1928.

First performance of "The Medium" was given on May 8,
1946, at Columbia University in New York. Claramae Turner participated in the world premiere.

May Ninth

> In Chopin's compositions boldness is always justified;
> richness, often exuberance, never interferes with clear-
> ness; singularity never degenerates into the uncouth and
> fantastic; the sculpturing is never disordered; the luxury
> of ornament never unloads the chaste eloquence of the
> principal lines. --Franz Liszt

An historic return at Carnegie Hall of Vladimer Horowitz
occurred on May 9, 1965.

Ezio Pinza died May 9, 1957.

Carla Maria Giulini was born May 9, 1914.

World premiere of Bruckner's First Symphony was presented
at Linz on May 9, 1868.

Frank Connor was born May 9, 1902.

Vittoria Tesi died May 9, 1775.

May Tenth

> In many respects Wagner resembles Napoleon III. Like
> him he always had faith in his work, notwithstanding
> the most adverse circumstances. All the means which
> could help him toward the goal of his aspirations he
> has employed with an energy which no musician has pos-
> sessed before him to the same degree.--Ferdinand
> Hiller

The Grand Festival March was composed by Wagner for the
opening of the Centennial Exhibition, Philadelphia on May 10,
1876.

Angelica Catalani was born May 10, 1780.

Nordica as Aïda.

Lillian Nordica died May 10, 1914.

Joaquin Nin Culmell's Suite from "El Burlandor de Seville" was given its premiere on May 10, 1967, by the San Francisco Symphony under the direction of Josef Krips.

Richard Lewis was born May 10, 1914.

Max Lorenz was born May 10, 1901.

May Eleventh

> The happiest genius will hardly succeed by nature and instinct alone in rising to the sublime. Art is art; he who has not thought it out has no right to call himself an artist. --Goethe

Ilma di Murska made her first appearance in London on May 11, 1865, in the title role of "Lucia di Lammermoor."

Max Reger died May 11, 1916.

Joseph Marx was born May 11, 1882.

Andrew Imbrie's First Symphony was given its premiere performance on May 11, 1966, by the San Francisco Symphony.

May Twelfth

> No art is more closely connected with the inner life of man than music, whose magic power steps in precisely at the point where the positive expression of language fails. --Ritter

Gabriel Faure was born May 12, 1845.

Frederick Smetana died May 12, 1884.

"L'Elisir d'Amore," composed by Donizetti for Erminia Frezzolini, was first performed on May 12, 1832.

Jules Massenet was born May 12, 1842.

Lillian Nordica was born May 12, 1857.

Eugene Ysaye died May 12, 1931.

Adolph von Henselt was born May 12, 1814.

May Thirteenth

> The older I become, so much the more clearly do I
> perceive how important it is first to learn, and then
> to form opinions--not the latter before the former;
> also not both at once. --Mendelssohn

Mendelssohn's Symphony No. 4 in A Major (Italian) was first
heard on May 13, 1833, in London with the composer conducting.

Antonio Pistocchi, virtuoso singer and teacher and founder
of the famous School of Singing at Bologna, died on May 13,
1726.

Sir Arthur Sullivan was born May 13, 1842.

Clara Louise Kellogg died May 13, 1916.

Hermann Levi died May 13, 1900.

May Fourteenth

> Artists, like the Greek Gods, are only revealed to one
> another. --Oscar Wilde

A surprise for London! Remarkable debut of Adelina Patti
at Covent Garden as Amina in "La Sonnambula" at the age
of eighteen, on May 14, 1861.

Patrice Munsel was born May 14, 1925.

Operatic debut of Jan Peerce took place on May 14, 1938,
in Philadelphia.

Otto Klemperer was born May 14, 1885.

Strauss' "Josephslegende" was first produced May 14, 1914,
in Paris.

Lucrezia Bori died May 14, 1960.

Seymour Lipkin was born May 14, 1927.

Emile Prudent died May 14, 1863.

Sigismond Stojowski was born May 14, 1869.

May Fifteenth

> The aim of art is not only to copy the examples of nature, but to beautify, to idealize, and to group and arrange them. --Ernst Pauer

Claudio Monteverdi was born May 15, 1567.

Michael William Balfe was born May 15, 1808.

Stephen Heller was born May 15, 1813.

First performance of Stravinsky's ballet "Pulcinella, " was presented by the Ballet Russe in Paris on May 15, 1920.

Covent Garden opened on May 15, 1858, with Meyerbeer's "Les Huguenots. "

May Sixteenth

> For recreation from your musical studies read the poets frequently. --Schumann

Teatro La Fenice in Venice was inaugurated May 16, 1792, when Gasparo Pacchierotti made his last public appearance.

Jan Kiepura was born May 16, 1902.

Richard Tauber was born May 16, 1892.

American Composers Alliance was founded on May 16, 1938.

Clemens Krauss died May 16, 1954.

May Seventeenth

> I will live alone and pour my pain with passion into
> music, where it turns to what is best within my better
> self.--George Eliot

Birgit Nilsson was born May 17, 1922.

First performance of Mascagni's "Cavallerio Rusticana" was
given on May 17, 1890, in Rome.

Erik Satie was born May 17, 1866.

Lilli Lehmann died May 17, 1929.

Olga Samaroff died May 17, 1948.

Fanny Cecile Mendelssohn Hensel died May 17, 1848.

Paul Dukas died May 17, 1935.

Zinka Milanov was born May 17, 1906.

Leonard Bernstein played his final concert as musical director of the New York Philharmonic on May 17, 1969.

Fausta Cleva was born May 17, 1902.

May Eighteenth

> Music is such a perfect expression of human emotion
> that we can almost deduce from it a moral science--
> a rule of life.--Goodrich

Clifford Curzon was born May 18, 1907.

Ezio Pinza was born May 18, 1892.

Gustav Mahler died May 18, 1911.

On May 18, 1897, Paul Dukas directed the first performance
of his "L'Apprenti Sorcier" (The Sorcerer's Apprentice) at a
Concert of the Societe Nationale in Paris.

Pauline Viardot-Garcia died May 18, 1910.

Isaac Albeniz died May 18, 1909.

First performance of Gluck's opera "Iphigenie en Tauride" took place on May 18, 1779, in Paris.

Milka Ternina died May 18, 1941.

Karl Goldmark was born May 18, 1830.

May Nineteenth

> Sing with your voices, and with your hearts, and with all your moral convictions, sing the new songs, not only with your tongue but with your life.--St. Augustine

Nellie Melba was born May 19, 1859.

World premiere of "Linda Di Chamounix" by Donizetti took place on May 19, 1842, in Vienna.

National Association for American Composers and Conductors was founded by Dr. Henry Hadley on May 19, 1933.

Rosina Storchio was born May 19, 1876.

May Twentieth

> The principal requisites for a musician, a fine ear and a swift power of comprehension, come, like all things, from above.--Robert Schumann

Clara Wieck Schumann died May 20, 1896.

Jerdy Fitelberg was born May 20, 1903.

First American performance of Beethoven's Ninth Symphony was given on May 20, 1846, by the New York Philharmonic Society in New York.

May Twenty-first

> A composer who has the power to construct very beautiful works of art in a certain form by inventing ideas, and by showing in a new light ideas not invented by him, deserves to be regarded as a great composer.--Engel

Premiere of Leoncavallo's opera "Pagliacci" took place in
Milan on May 21, 1892, with Toscanini conducting.   The
first cast included Victor Maurel and Mario Ancona.

Gina Bachauer was born May 21, 1913.

Alexander Fried was born May 21, 1902.

Franz von Suppe died May 21, 1895.

Amy Fay was born May 21, 1844.

May Twenty-second

> To Wagner at birth the Gods gave two gifts--a capacity
> to receive and to retain the most various and the most
> intense impressions, and, as he phrases it, 'the ever
> intensified spirit that ever seeks new things.'--Dann-
> reuther

Richard Wagner was born May 22, 1813.

The corner-stone of Wagner's theatre in Bayreuth was laid
on May 22, 1872.

Verdi conducted the first performance of his "Requiem" on
May 22, 1874, in Milan.

Henriette Sontag chose Rossini's "Semiramide" for her farewell to the operatic stage on May 22, 1830, in Berlin.   However, years later she returned to the stage.

Mendelssohn's "Paulus" was first performed May 22, 1836,
in Dusseldorf.

John Browning was born May 22, 1933.

May Twenty-third

> Beethoven rose so far above his fellowmen that he saw
> seas and countries, yes, suns and stars, which we can-
> not yet behold. --Merz

First performance of Beethoven's opera "Fidelio" in its
final form was given on May 23, 1814, in Vienna.

Rosa Raisa was born May 23, 1893.

Jean Baptiste Viotti was born May 23, 1753.

American premiere of "Don Giovanni" was given on May 23, 1826, with the Garcias--the elder Manuel as the Don, and the younger Manuel as Leporello; the elder Manuel's wife was Donna Elvira, and his daughter Maria (later the famous Malibran) was Zerlina.

May Twenty-fourth

> So that genius exists, it matters little how it appears, whether in the depths, as with Bach; on the heights, as with Mozart; or in the depths and on the heights at once, as with Beethoven. --Schumann

Overture to Goethe's "Egmont," composed by Beethoven, was first performed at the Hofburg Theatre in Vienna on May 24, 1810.

Marietta Piccolomina made her English debut in the London premiere of "La Traviata" on May 24, 1856, at Her Majesty's, while, at Covent Garden, the equally charming Angiolina Bosio was soon rivaling her in the same role.

Nellie Melba made her London debut as Lucia on May 24, 1888.

On May 24, 1960, the Glyndebourne Festival Opera opened its season with a revival of "I Puritani." Vittorio Gui conducted and the cast included Joan Sutherland and Monica Sinclair.

Elgar's Second Symphony was first heard on May 24, 1911, in London.

Sasha Gorodnitzki was born May 24, 1905.

Claudia Muzio died May 24, 1936.

May Twenty-fifth

> The masterworks of the past should be the standard of the works of the present. --Franz

Camille Erlanger was born May 25, 1863.

First performance of "H.M.S. Pinafore," one of the most
popular of all light operas, was given at the Opera Comique
Theatre in London on May 25, 1878.

Edouard De Reszke died May 25, 1917.

Mischa Levitzki was born May 25, 1898.

Gustav Holst died May 25, 1934.

May Twenty-sixth

There are many things in music which must be imagined
without being heard. It is the intelligent hearers who
are endowed with that imagination whom we should en-
deavor to please especially. --C. P. E. Bach

Eugene Goosens was born May 26, 1893.

World premiere of "Le Rossignol" by Stravinsky was presented in Paris on May 26, 1914, with Pierre Monteux conducting.

Teresa Stratas was born May 26, 1938.

Victor Herbert died May 26, 1924.

Inge Borkh was born May 26, 1917.

May Twenty-seventh

The one thing you have to do is to make a clear-voiced
little instrument of yourself, which other people can de-
pend upon entirely for the note wanted. --Ruskin

Joseph Joachim, at the age of thirteen, played Beethoven's
Concerto in D Major for Violin and Orchestra on May 27,
1844, with Mendelssohn conducting.

Niccolo Paganini died May 27, 1840.

Giuditta Pasta died May 27, 1840.

Paganini, seen here in prison,
died May 27, 1840.

Maurice Ravel made his debut as an orchestral conductor
with the Societe National, May 27, 1899, performing his
own Overture, "Scheherazade," from manuscript.

Mario Del Monaco was born May 27, 1915.

Egon Petri died May 27, 1962.

Jacques Halevy was born May 27, 1799.

Anton Raaf died May 27, 1797.

May Twenty-eighth

> Art springs in its earliest beginnings from religion, and
> returns to it in its highest development. --Ambros

Leopold Mozart died May 28, 1787.

Thomas Moore was born May 28, 1779.

Luigi Boccherini died May 28, 1805.

Gigli's first appearance in London took place on May 28,
1930, at Covent Garden in "Andrea Chenier," his favorite
role.

Dietrich Fischer-Dieskau was born May 28, 1925.

First performance of Paul Hindemith's opera "Mathis der
Maler" was given on May 28, 1938, in Zurich.   Robert
Denzler conducted the premiere.

Riccardo Zandonai was born May 28, 1883.

Victor Nessler died May 28, 1890.

The revival of "Les Hugenots" was presented at La Scala on
May 28, 1962.   The cast included Joan Sutherland, Franco
Corelli and Giorgio Tozzi.

May Twenty-ninth

> Perfection should be the aim of every true artist. --
> Beethoven

Anna Milder-Hauptmann died May 29, 1838.

"Sacre du Printemps," composed by Igor Stravinsky, was
heard for the first time on May 29, 1913, in Paris.

Mily Balakirev died May 29, 1910.

Isaac Albeniz was born May 29, 1860.

Erich Wolfgang Korngold was born May 29, 1897.

Zubin Mehta was born May 29, 1936.

New York Philharmonic Promenade Concerts were inaugurated on May 29, 1963.

Mario Chamlee was born May 29, 1892.

May Thirtieth

> It is cheering once more to meet an artist (Moscheles) who is not a victim to envy, jealousy, or miserable egotism. --Mendelssohn

Ignaz Moscheles was born May 30, 1794.

World premiere of "The Bartered Bride" was given at the National Theater in Prague on May 30, 1866.

George London was born May 30, 1920.

Last public appearance of Caffarelli took place in Naples on May 30, 1754.

First London performance of "Die Meistersinger" was given on May 30, 1882, under the direction of Hans Richter.

Stravinsky's "Oedipus Rex" was first heard on May 30, 1927, in Paris.

May Thirty-first

> But God has a few of us whom he
>   whispers in the ear;
> The rest may reason and welcome: 'tis we
>   musicians know. --
>
>   Robert Browning

Franz Joseph Haydn died May 31, 1809.

Frances Alda was born May 31, 1883.

Alfred Deller was born May 31, 1912.

Alfredo Antonini was born May 31, 1901.

Raoul Gunsbourg died May 31, 1955.

JUNE

The love of beauty is taste; the
creation of beauty is art. --Emerson

June First

What is music? The very existence of music is wonderful, I might even say miraculous. Its domain is between thought and phenomena. Like a twilight mediator,
it hovers between spirit and matter, related to both, yet
differing from each. It is spirit, but spirit subject to
the measurement of time; it is matter, but matter that
can dispense with space. --Heine

Mark Hambourg was born June 1, 1879.

Franz Liszt gave his first concert at the age of thirteen on
June 1, 1824, in London.

Michael Glinka was born June 1, 1804.

Sigrid Onegin was born June 1, 1891.

Josef Pleyel, composer and founder of the piano factory in
Paris, was born June 1, 1757.

Friedrich Bechstein, founder of a celebrated firm of piano
makers, was born June 1, 1826.

Werner Janssen was born June 1, 1900.

June Second

If our art is not to sink entirely to the level of trade,
commerce, and fashion, the training for it must be complete, intelligent and really artistic. --Merz

Nicolas Rubinstein was born June 2, 1835.

Felix von Weingartner was born June 2, 1863.

Manuel Del Popolo Garcia died June 2, 1832.

Sir Edward Elgar was born June 2, 1857.

Premiere performance of "Lulu" took place on June 2, 1937, in Zurich.   The conductor was Robert Denzler.

June Third

> The Realistic is the truth, a close copy of nature.   The
> Ideal is what a man wishes were true. --Van Cleve

George Bizet died June 3, 1875, just three months after the premiere of "Carmen. "

Johann Strauss (the Younger) died June 3, 1899.

Jan Peerce was born June 3, 1904.

American Musicological Society was founded on June 3, 1934.

June Fourth

> The greater the advances we make in art the less we
> are satisfied with our works of an early date. --
> Beethoven

Robert Merrill was born June 4, 1917.

Fedora Barbieri was born June 4, 1920.

Stanislaw Moniuszko died June 4, 1872.

Serge Koussevitzky died in Boston on June 4, 1951.

First American performance of Sibelius' Symphonic Poem "Oceanides" took place June 4, 1914, in an all-Sibelius program with the composer conducting.

June Fifth

> There never lived a musician more German than thou.
> England renders thee justice, France admires thee, but
> Germany alone can love thee.--Richard Wagner (at Von
> Weber's grave)

Carl Maria von Weber died June 5, 1826.

Orlando Gibbons died June 5, 1625.

The ballet "Daphnis et Chloe" by Maurice Ravel, was first
produced on June 5, 1912, at the Chatelet Theatre in Paris.
Pierre Monteux conducted.

Sir Julius Benedict died June 5, 1885.

Johann Kuhnau died June 5, 1722.

Ricardo Zandonai died June 5, 1944.

June Sixth

> Wouldst thou know if a people be well governed, if its
> laws be good or bad, examine the music it practices.
> --Confucius

Siegfried Wagner was born June 6, 1869.

Philippe Entremont was born June 6, 1934.

Aram Khatchaturian was born June 6, 1903.

Henri Vieuxtemps died June 6, 1881.

Arthur Mendel was born June 6, 1905.

Marietta Brambilla was born June 6, 1807.

First performance of Gustav Mahler's (unfinished) Tenth
Symphony was given June 6, 1924, in Prague.

Vincent Persichetti was born June 6, 1915.

June Seventh

> Art, as far as it has the ability, follows nature, as a
> pupil imitates his master, so that art must be, as it
> were, a descendent of God. --Dante

Leopold Auer was born June 7, 1845.

Maria Malibran made her operatic debut in London on June
7, 1825, as Rosina in "Il Barbieri di Siviglia."

Marcella Sembrich made her first appearance on the operatic
stage in Athens in "I Puritani" on June 7, 1877.

Georg Szell was born June 7, 1897.

Boris Goldovsky was born June 7, 1908.

Emil Paur died June 7, 1932.

June Eighth

> I am inclined to think that only men of genius understand
> each other fully and thoroughly. --Schumann

Robert Schumann was born June 8, 1810.

Memorable final curtain at Covent Garden for Nellie Melba
on June 8, 1926.

Luigi Ricci was born June 8, 1805.

Alberto Jonas was born June 8, 1868.

Tomasco Albinoni was born June 8, 1671.

Frederick Shepherd Converse died June 8, 1940.

June Ninth

> Time goes on, and what suffices for one age appears to
> the next as a woeful shortcoming. --Beethoven

World premiere of Britten's opera "The Burning Fiery Furnace" took place on June 9, 1966.

Carl Otto Nicolai was born June 9, 1810.

Heinrich Finck died June 9, 1527.

Philippe de Vitry died June 9, 1361.

Louis Gruenberg died June 9, 1964.

Carl Nielsen was born June 9, 1865.

London Symphony Orchestra gave its first concert on June 9, 1904. Hans Richter conducted.

June Tenth

> It is often by seeing and hearing musical works (operas and other good musical compositions), rather than by rules, that taste is formed.--Rameau

First performance of "Tristan Und Isolde" took place on June 10, 1865, in Munich. The Tristan and Isolde of the world premiere were husband and wife: Ludwig Schnorr von Carolsfeld and Malwine Schnorr von Carolsfeld. Hans von Bulow conducted.

Titto Ruffo, one of the greatest baritones of all times, was born on June 10, 1877.

Ralph Kirkpatrick was born June 10, 1911.

Ernest Chausson died June 10, 1899.

Frederick Delius died June 10, 1934.

Arrigo Boito died June 10, 1918.

Frederick Michael Kalkbrenner died on June 10, 1849.

June Eleventh

> For Orpheus's lute was strong with poets' sinews,
> Whose golden touch could soften steel and stones.--
>   Shakespeare

Rise Stevens was born June 11, 1913.

Richard Strauss was born June 11, 1864.

First London performance of Gounod's "Faust" took place on June 11, 1863.   Luigi Arditi conducted.

Anna Mehlig was born June 11, 1846.

Geoffrey Toye died June 11, 1942.

June Twelfth

If we look around in modern music we will find that we have a terrible deal of mind and astonishingly few ideas. --Ambros

Angelica Catalini died June 12, 1849.

Teresa Carreno died June 12, 1917.

Sigma Alpha Iota, National Music Fraternity, established at University School of Music, Ann Arbor, Michigan June 12, 1903.

Edward Horsley died June 12, 1858.

Carlisle Floyd was born June 12, 1926.

World premiere of Gustav Mahler's Third Symphony took place in Crefeld, Germany on June 12, 1902, with the composer conducting.

Werner Josten was born June 12, 1888.

June Thirteenth

By the word 'symphony' we designate the largest proportion hitherto attained in instrumental music. -- Schumann

Stravinsky's "Petrouchka" was first produced on June 13, 1911, in Paris.

Elisabeth Schumann was born June 13, 1888.

Edvard Poldini was born June 13, 1869.

Carlos Chavez was born June 13, 1899.

Eugene Goossens died June 13, 1962.

June Fourteenth

> The greatest beauties of melody and harmony become
> faults and imperfections when they are not in their
> proper place.--Gluck

Orlando di Lasso, Musician to the Duke of Bavaria, died in
Munich on June 14, 1594.

John McCormack was born June 14, 1884.

Cristobal Morales died June 14, 1553.

First performance of "The Red Poppy" ballet by Gliere was
presented June 14, 1927.

June Fifteenth

> That music is the usefulest which makes the best words
> most beautiful, which enchants them in our memory,
> each with its own glory of sound, and which applies
> them closest to the heart on the moment we need them.
> --Ruskin

Edvard Grieg was born June 15, 1843.

Ernestine Schumann-Heink was born June 15, 1861.

Alfred Cortot died June 15, 1962.

Otto Luening was born June 15, 1900.

Max Rudolf was born June 15, 1902.

Louis Claude Daquin died June 15, 1772.

First American performance of "I Pagliacci" was given on

June 15, 1893, in New York.

Robert Russell Bennett was born June 15, 1894.

Johanna Gadski was born June 15, 1872.

June Sixteenth

> If by your art you cannot please all, content the few.
> To please the multitude is bad. --Schumann

Johann Adam Hiller died June 16, 1804.

New World premiere of "La Tosca" was presented on June 16, 1900, at the Teatro Colon, Buenos Aires.

Otto Jahn was born June 16, 1813.

At Glyndebourne, on June 16, 1967, Cavalli's "Ormindo" was given first known production since the year 1644.

Antonin Dvorak was awarded an honorary music doctorate by Cambridge University on June 16, 1891.

Sigrid Onegin died June 16, 1943.

June Seventeenth

> Doing easily what others find difficult is talent; doing what is impossible for talent is genius. --Amiel

Igor Stravinsky was born June 17, 1882.

Charles Gounod was born June 17, 1818.

Henriette Sontag died June 17, 1854.

Victor Maurel was born June 17, 1848.

Hermann Reutter was born June 17, 1900.

June Eighteenth

> How very differently does he create whose inner ear is
> judge of the ideas which he simultaneously conceives
> and criticizes! This mental ear grasps and holds fast
> the musical vision, and is a divine secret belonging to
> music alone, incomprehensible to the layman. --Von
> Weber

Premiere of Weber's "Der Freischutz" was given on June
18, 1821, in Berlin. Weber conducted the triumphant debut.

Katherine Goodson was born June 18, 1872.

First American performance of Donizetti's "L'Elisir d'Amore"
was given June 18, 1838.

June Nineteenth

> The works of all beginners teem with reminiscences:
> every composition reveals the model form from which
> it is derived; and it is only much later that they learn
> to act independently, and to strive for the ideal. --
>   Von Weber

Ferdinand David was born June 19, 1810.

Elgar's Enigma Variations were first performed on June 19,
1899, in London.

June Twentieth

> And ever against eating cares
> Lap me in soft Lydian airs,
> Married to immortal verse
> Such as the melting soul may pierce,
> Untwisting all the chains that tie
> The hidden soul of harmony. --
>
>   Milton

Helen Traubel was born June 20, 1899.

Jaques Offenbach was born June 20, 1819.

Josef and Rosina Lhevinne were married on June 20, 1898.

World premiere of Donizetti's opera, "L'Elisir d'Amore," was produced in Paris June 20, 1831.

First London performance of "Tristan und Isolde" was given on June 20, 1882, with Hans Richter conducting.

Jeanette Scovotti made her debut at Vienna Volksoper on June 20, 1966, singing the title role in "Lucia di Lammermoor."

June Twenty-first

> The world is full of musical treasures, but we are not being enriched by these to half the extent we ought to be. --Booth

Premiere of Wagner's "Die Meistersinger von Nürnberg" took place in Munich on June 21, 1868, with Von Bulow conducting.

Hermann Scherchen was born June 21, 1891.

Nikolai Rimsky-Korsakov died June 21, 1908.

First performance of Richard Strauss' tone poem "Tod und Verklarung" was given on June 21, 1890.

Karl F. Curschmann was born June 21, 1804.

June Twenty-second

> Music resembles poetry: in each
> Are nameless graces which no methods teach,
> And which a master hand alone can reach. --
>
> Pope

Theodor Leschetizky was born June 22, 1830.

The London premiere of "Aida" was given on June 22, 1876, with Adelina Patti, Ernest Nicolini, Sofia Scalchi and Antonio Cotogni.

Jennie Tourel was born June 22, 1910.

Frank Damrosch was born June 22, 1859.

Albert Carre, author of several libretti, was born June 22, 1852.

June Twenty-third

> Hats off, gentlemen! a genius!--Schumann, in reference to Chopin

Chopin gave a concert in London June 23, 1848.   "After the hammer and tongs in the piano to which we have of late years been accustomed, the delicacy of Chopin's touch is delicious to the ear." (Chorley's criticism)

Mieczyslaw Horszowski was born June 23, 1892.

Carl Reinecke was born June 23, 1824.

Marietta Alboni died June 23, 1894.

Kenneth McKellar was born June 23, 1927.

Antonio Bernacchi, famous castrato singer who appeared in several of Handel's operas, was born June 23, 1685.

June Twenty-fourth

> It is only in original work that genius ripens to maturity. --Richard Wagner

Goossens' "Don Juan de Manara" was first produced on June 24, 1937, in London.

The Handel Opera Society of London presented Handel's "Rodelinda" on June 24, 1959, with Joan Sutherland in the title role.

Pierre Fournier was born June 24, 1906.

The American Conservatory of Music at Fountainbleau, France, was inaugurated on June 24, 1921.

June Twenty-fifth

> I hope you will like my 'Lobesang' or 'Song of Praise.'
> It is a kind of universal thanksgiving on the words of the
> last psalm: 'Let everything that hath breath praise the
> Lord.'   The instruments begin with a symphony of three
> movements, and the voices take it up and continue it
> with different words, solos and choruses, till all unite
> again in the same words. --Mendelssohn

Mendelssohn's "Song of Praise" was performed for the first
time on June 25, 1840, at the celebration of the fourth centenary of printing.

On June 25, 1886, Arturo Toscanini conducted publicly for
the first time at the age of nineteen in the performance of
Verdi's "Aida" in Rio de Janeiro.

Gustave Charpentier was born June 25, 1860.

Rafael Joseffy died June 25, 1915.

E. T. A. Hoffmann died June 25, 1822.

First performance of Stravinsky's "Firebird Orchestral
Suite" was presented June 25, 1910, in Paris.

U.S. premiere on June 25, 1967, of Britten's "The Burning
Fiery Furnace" at Caramoor, Katonah.

George Philipp Teleman died June 25, 1767.

June Twenty-sixth

> The human voice is really the foundation of all music;
> and whatever the development of the art, whatever the
> boldest combinations of a composer or the most brilliant
> execution of a virtuoso, in the end they must always re-
> turn to the standard set by vocal music. --Wagner

Richard Crooks was born June 26, 1900.

Serge Koussevitzky was born June 26, 1874.

World premiere of Wagner's "Die Walkure" took place on
June 26, 1870, in Munich.   Franz Wullner conducted.

Frieda Hempel was born June 26, 1885.

Leonid Hambro was born June 26, 1920.

First performance given of Gustav Mahler's Ninth Symphony
on June 26, 1912, in Vienna under the direction of Bruno
Walter.

June Twenty-seventh

> Art is not for the end of getting riches.   Only become
> a greater and a greater artist; the rest will come of
> itself. --Schumann

Anna Moffo was born June 27, 1934.

Toti Dal Monte was born June 27, 1899.

Albert Loschorn was born June 27, 1819.

John Pyke Hullah was born June 27, 1812.

World premiere of De Bussy's cantata, "L'Enfant prodigue, "
was presented in Paris on June 27, 1884.

June Twenty-eighth

> Freedom of spirit and expression are not possible but
> with nimbleness and sureness of the fingers. --Von Weber

Josef Joachim was born June 28, 1831.

Luisa Tetrazzini was born June 28, 1871.

Jean Jaques Rousseau was born June 28, 1712.

Carlotta Marchisio died June 28, 1872.

June Twenty-ninth

> When technique, already faultless, is qualified by re-
> finement and poetry in touch and taste, it ceases to be
> simply mechanical and becomes artistic. --Christiani

Ignaz Paderewski died June 29, 1941.

Rafael Kubelik was born June 29, 1914.

Beethoven's "Missa Solemnis" was first performed in its entirety on June 29, 1830, at Warnsdorf, Bohemia.

Maria Malibran and Giulia Grisi appeared together for the first time on June 29, 1835, singing a duet from "Semiramide" at a concert in London.

Nelson Eddy was born June 29, 1901.

Nikolai Rimsky-Korsakov conducted a concert of Russian music at the World Exhibition in Paris on June 29, 1889.

June Thirtieth

> Music, in the best sense, does not require novelty; nay the older it is, and the more accustomed to it, the greater its effect. --Goethe

Teresa Stolz made her farewell appearance at La Scala on June 30, 1879, in the "Manzoni" Requiem.

Italo Campanini was born June 30, 1845.

Georg Benda was born June 30, 1722.

Sergei Rachmaninoff completed his Third Symphony on June 30, 1936.

JULY

Beauty is visible harmony. --<u>Aristotle</u>

July First

> Don't be afraid of the words 'theory,' 'thorough-bass,' 'counterpoint,' etc., they will meet you half way if you do the same. --<u>Schumann</u>

Wilhelm Friedemann Bach died July 1, 1784.

Manuel Patricio Garcia died July 1, 1906.

Eric Satie died July 1, 1925.

Pierre Monteux died July 1, 1964.

Hans Werner Henze was born July 1, 1926.

July Second

> The sole aim of the composer should be the progress of his art. --<u>Gluck</u>

Christoph Willibald von Gluck was born July 2, 1714.

Ludwig Schnorr, German tenor who became the first Tristan, was born July 2, 1836.

Felix Mottl died July 2, 1911.

Christoph Willibald von Gluck,
born July 2, 1714.
Painting by J. S. Duplessis,
Imperial Gallery, Vienna.

July Third

As the true poem is the poet's mind, so true expression
is the artist's soul. --Tapper

Ethel Newcomb died July 3, 1959.

Rafael Joseffy was born July 3, 1852.

Leos Janacek was born July 3, 1854.

Deems Taylor died July 3, 1966.

Theodore Presser was born July 3, 1848.

July Fourth

A musician's highest aim is to apply his powers to religious music. --Schumann

William Byrd died July 4, 1623.

Stephen Foster was born July 4, 1826.

Louis Claude Daquin was born July 4, 1694.

July Fifth

Pianistic technique implies, in its widest sense, a faultless mastery of every mechanical difficulty in the required tempo, and without any perceptible effort. --Christiani

Wanda Landowska was born July 5, 1877.   "In everything that she touched she showed herself a complete artist."

Jan Kubelik was born July 5, 1880.

Titta Ruffo died in Florence on the night of July 5, 1953.

July Sixth

The spirit of the artist is one of self-abnegation, of devotion to ideal aims. --Fillmore

Vladimir Ashkenazy was born July 6, 1936.

Outstanding performance of "Don Giovanni" was given at Covent Garden on July 6, 1861, with Giulia Grisi, Adelina Patti, Jean-Baptiste Faure and Enrico Tamberlik.

Dorothy Kirsten was born July 6, 1917.

Eugene List was born July 6, 1918.

Emile Jaques-Dalcroze was born July 6, 1865, in Vienna.

Philippe Gaubert was born July 6, 1879.

July Seventh

Contrast, not uniformity, is a condition of every work of art. --Christiani

Gian Carlo Menotti was born July 7, 1911.

Gustav Mahler was born July 7, 1860.

Jean Casadesus was born July 7, 1927.

First performance of Handel's "Utrecht Te Deum" was given July 7, 1713, in London.

July Eighth

Ye peddlers in art, do ye not sink into the earth when ye are reminded of the words uttered by Beethoven on his dying bed: 'I believe I am yet but at the beginning.' --Schumann

The degree of Doctor of Music was conferred on Haydn on July 8, 1791, by the University of Oxford.

Percy Grainger was born July 8, 1882.

Berkshire Music Center inaugurated at Lenox, Massachusetts on July 8, 1940, under the general direction of Serge Koussevitzky.

Philippe Gaubert died July 8, 1941.

July Ninth

The purest music will produce the purest sentiments. How important, then, that we should study the best!-- Merz

Leonard Pennario was born July 9, 1924.

Ania Dorfmann was born July 9, 1899.

Marianne Brandt died July 9, 1921.

Otterino Respighi was born July 9, 1879.

The Marchissio sisters, Carlotta and Barbara, performed in "Semiramide" in Paris on July 9, 1860. Napoleon III, Empress Eugenie and the whole court were in the audience.

David Diamond was born July 9, 1915.

Richard Hageman was born July 9, 1882.

July Tenth

Music is the outflow of a beautiful mind. --Schumann

The British premiere of "Madame Butterfly" took place at Covent Garden on July 10, 1905. A brilliant performance with Emmy Destinn, Enrico Caruso and Antonio Scotti.

Henri Wieniawski was born July 10, 1835.

Hugo Riemann died July 10, 1919.

Sir Donald Francis Tovey died July 10, 1940.

Rosalyn Tureck inaugurated the Bach Society sessions at Lincoln Center on July 10, 1967.

Carl Orff was born July 10, 1895.

Ludwig Fischer died July 10, 1825.

July Eleventh

Lightlier move
The minutes edged with music. --

Tennyson

George Gershwin died July 11, 1937.

Edwin Stringham was born July 11, 1890.

Mattiwilda Dobbs was born July 11, 1937.

Joseph Tichatschek was born July 11, 1807.

Anton Rubinstein made his debut as a pianist July 11, 1839, in Moscow.

Anton Rubinstein's debut as a pianist
was in Moscow on July 11, 1839.

Nicolai Gedda was born July 11, 1925.

July Twelfth

The best definition of true melody, in a higher sense,
is something that may be sung.--Ernst Hoffmann

Kirsten Flagstad was born July 12, 1895.

Van Cliburn was born July 12, 1934.

Clara Louise Kellogg was born July 12, 1842.

Pol Plancon was born July 12, 1854.

July Thirteenth

> All the arts flow from the same source. It is the idea
> embodied in a work of art, and not the mode of enun-
> ciating it, that determines its rank in the scale of
> beauty.--Franz Liszt

Arnold Schoenberg died July 13, 1951.

Carlo Bergonzi was born July 13, 1924.

First Festival of Pan-American Chamber Music opened at
Mexico City on July 13, 1937.

July Fourteenth

> From the bottom of my heart do I detest that one-
> sidedness of the uneducated many who think that their
> own small vocation is the best, and that every other is
> a humbug.--Schubert

Jacob Stainer was born July 14, 1621.

Alexander Kopylov was born July 14, 1854.

Nadia Reisenberg was born July 14, 1905.

William Mason died July 14, 1908.

July Fifteenth

> Three trifles are essential for a good piano or singing
> teacher: the finest feeling, the deepest feeling, the
> most delicate ear, and in addition the requisite knowl-
> edge, energy and some practice.--Frederich Wieck

Karl Czerny died July 15, 1857.

Leopold Auer died July 15, 1930.

Lawrence Tibbett died July 15, 1960.

Giuditta Pasta sang "Semiramide" at its first performance in London on July 15, 1824, at the King's Theatre, under Rossini's direction.

Ernest Bloch died July 15, 1959.

Carlo Farinelli died July 15, 1782.

Alfred Hertz was born July 15, 1872.

July Sixteenth

> Strange, that one should feel major and minor as opposites. They both present the same face, now more joyous, now more serious; a mere touch of the brush suffices to turn the one into the other.--Busoni

Fannie Bloomfield-Zeisler was born July 16, 1863.

Eugene Ysaye was born July 16, 1858.

Fritz Mahler was born July 16, 1901.

July Seventeenth

> True art endures forever, and the true artist delights in the works of great minds.--Beethoven

Handel's "Water Music" was first performed on the Thames, July 17, 1717.

Karl Tausig died July 17, 1871.

Therese Tietjens was born July 17, 1831.

Eduard Remenyi was born July 17, 1830.

Eleanor Steber was born July 17, 1916.

Sir Donald Francis Tovey was born on July 17, 1875.

July Eighteenth

> She (Viardot) abandons herself to inspiration with that
> easy simplicity which gives everything an air of gran-
> deur.... She possesses in a word, the great secret of
> artists: before expressing something, she feels it.
> She does not listen to her voice but to her heart. --
> De Musset

Pauline Viardot Garcia was born July 18, 1821.

Giovanni Battista Bononcini was born July 18, 1670.

Hugo Riemann was born July 18, 1849.

Ferdinand David died July 18, 1873.

July Nineteenth

> The love of the beautiful, next to the spiritual percep-
> tion of God and eternal relationships, must be admitted
> to be man's crowning distinction. --Van Cleve

Louis Kentner was born July 19, 1905.

Alfredo Catalani was born July 19, 1854.

Joseph Masart was born July 19, 1811.

Ludwig van Beethoven met the German poet, Wolfgang von
Goethe on July 19, 1812, at Teplitz, Bohemia.

Franz Liszt appeared for the last time in a public concert
on July 19, 1886.

July Twentieth

> It is essential that you train your mind more than your
> fingers. --Moscheles

Ernest Hutcheson was born July 20, 1871.

Henry B. Tremaine was born July 20, 1866.

First performance of Schoenberg's "Serenade" was given on

July 20, 1924, in Donaveschingen, Germany.

July Twenty-first

> The instrument on which he played
> Was in Cremonas' workshop made,
> By a great master of the past
> Ere yet was lost the art divine;
> . . . .
> Exquisite was it in design,
> Perfect in each minutest part,
> A marvel of the lutist's art;
> And in its hollow chamber, thus,
> The maker from whose hands it came
> Had written his unrivalled name,
>   'Antonius Stradivarius'--   Longfellow

Isaac Stern was born July 21, 1920.

Mary Anne Paton died July 21, 1864.

Johann Nepomuk Maelzel died July 21, 1838, at sea, on his way to the United States.

Ludwig Schnorr died July 21, 1865.

July Twenty-second

> The style of a writer is almost always the faithful representative of his mind. Therefore, if any man wishes to write a clear style let him begin by making his thoughts clear, and if any would write a noble style let him first possess a noble soul. --Goethe

Julius Stockhausen was born July 22, 1826.

Licia Albanese was born July 22, 1913.

On July 22, 1865, Pauline Lucca, whom Meyerbeer himself coached in the part of Selika, sang in "L'Africane" at Covent Garden.

Luigi Arditi was born July 22, 1822.

Falla's "El Sombrero de tres Picos" was first produced on

July 22, 1919, in London.

July Twenty-third

> Freedom and progress are our true aim in the world of
> art, just as in the great creation at large. --Beethoven

Domenico Scarlatti died July 23, 1757.

Leon Fleisher was born July 23, 1928.

July Twenty-fourth

> He who sets limits to himself will always be expected
> to remain within them. --Schumann

Ernest Bloch was born July 24, 1880.

Benedetto Marcello was born July 24, 1686, and died July
24, 1739, his fifty-third birthday.

Ruggiero Ricci was born July 24, 1920.

Maurice Renaud was born July 24, 1861.

Peter Serkin was born July 24, 1947.

Julie Rive-King died July 24, 1937.

Giuseppe Di Stefano was born July 24, 1921.

July Twenty-fifth

> To accompany well you must not only be a good musi-
> cian, but you must be mesmeric, sympathetic, intuitive.
> --Haweis

Marcel Journet was born July 25, 1867.

Gianandrea Gavazzeni was born July 25, 1909.

Alfredo Casella was born July 25, 1883.

Agostino Steffani was born July 25, 1654.

Rosina Storchio died July 25, 1945.

July Twenty-sixth

> Music resembles chess: the queen (melody) has the
> most power, but the king (harmony) turns the scale.--
> Robert Schumann

John Field was born July 26, 1782.

World premiere of "Parsifal" took place on July 26, 1882,
in Bayreuth. Hermann Levi was the conductor.

Ernest Schelling was born July 26, 1876.

Alexis Weissenberg was born July 26, 1929.

Francesco Cilea was born July 26, 1866.

July Twenty-seventh

> Lose no opportunity of playing music--duos, trios, etc.
> --with others. This will make your playing broader
> and more flowing.--Schumann

Ferruccio Busoni died July 27, 1924.

Vladimar de Pachman was born July 27, 1848.

Ernst von Dohnanyi was born July 27, 1877.

Johann Philipp Kirnberger died July 27, 1783.

Harl McDonald was born July 27, 1899.

Mario Del Monaco was born July 27, 1915.

July Twenty-eighth

> Under heaven there is but one thing we ought to bow to
> --genius; and only one thing before which we ought to
> kneel--goodness.--Victor Hugo

Johann Sebastian Bach died July 28, 1750.

Antonio Vivaldi died July 28, 1741.

"Grisi's voice is deliciously pure and young, and she sings as if she loves her art and has its resources at her feet." (Chorley criticism). Giulia Grisi was born July 28, 1811.

The first London performance of "La Sonnambula" was given on July 28, 1831, with Pasta and Rubini of the original cast.

The "Bach Gesellschaft" was founded on July 28, 1850.

July Twenty-ninth

> Be sure the works of mighty men,
>   The good, the faithful, the sublime,
>   Stored in the gallery of Time,
> Repose awhile--to wake again.--
>
>   Goethe

Robert Schumann died July 29, 1856.

Enrique Granados was born July 29, 1867.

Sophie Mentor was born July 29, 1846.

July Thirtieth

> When I sat at my old worm-eaten piano I envied no king in his happiness.--Haydn

Grant Johannesen was born July 30, 1921.

Benjamin James Dale died July 30, 1943.

First American performance of Ferdinand David's "Festival March" took place in New York on July 30, 1874, under the direction of Theodore Thomas.

July Thirty-first

> Liszt will certainly be known in the history of pianoforte music as the greatest virtuoso of his time.--Fillmore

Franz Liszt died July 31, 1886.

Franz Liszt,
"greatest virtuoso of his time."
From a painting by Ary Scheffer.

AUGUST

It was by music that mankind
was harmonized.--Herder

August First

Every day that we spend without learning something is
a day lost.--Beethoven

Antonio Cotogni was born August 1, 1831.

William Steinberg was born August 1, 1899.

Arne's masque "Alfred" (in which occurs "Rule Britannia")
was first produced on August 1, 1740, in Cliveden, Bucking-
hamshire.

Oscar Hammerstein died August 1, 1919.

August Second

Among the various things which are suitable for man's
recreation and pleasure, music is the first and leads
us to the belief that it is a gift of God set apart for
this purpose.--Calvin

Enrico Caruso, most famous tenor of his time, died August
2, 1921.

Sir Arthur Bliss was born August 2, 1891.

First Festival of the International Society for Contemporary
Music opened at Salzburg on August 2, 1923.

Pietro Mascagni died August 2, 1945.

Marvin David Levy was born August 2, 1932.

August Third

> What St. Peter's or the Colosseum is to Rome, the
> Ponte Vecchio to Florence and the Grand Canal to Ven-
> ice, the Teatro alla Scalla is to Milan.....La Scala,
> Italy's proudest opera house, bows to no other company
> in the world.

The Teatro alla Scalla was opened on August 3, 1778 with
an opera by Antonio Salieri called "L'Europa Riconosciuta."

It was in "La Gioconda," at the Roman Arena, on August 3,
1947, that Maria Callas made the international debut that
launched her triumphant career. In the cast with her on
that occasion was Richard Tucker, who was making his Italian debut.

The Paris Conservatory was founded on August 3, 1795.

Rossini's "William Tell" was first performed on August 3,
1829. This was Rossini's last opera.

Louis Gruenberg was born August 3, 1884.

August Fourth

> Give me the best piano in Europe, and listeners who
> understand nothing and who do not sympathize with me
> in what I am doing--I no longer feel any pleasure. --
> Mozart

Wolfgang Amadeus Mozart and Constanze Weber were married
August 4, 1782.

Siegfried Wagner died August 4, 1930.

Jess Thomas was born August 4, 1928.

Italo Montemezzi was born August 4, 1875.

Gabriella Tucci was born August 4, 1932.

Alberto Franchetti died August 4, 1942.

William Howard Schuman was born August 4, 1910.

August Fifth

> Art is long, life short; judgment difficult, opportunity transient. --Goethe

Charles Ambroise Thomas was born August 5, 1811.

Erich Kleiber was born August 5, 1890.

Sebastien Erard died August 5, 1831.

August Sixth

> He who can see good in art-works is an abler and a far superior critic than he who sees only faults. --Merz

Eduard Hanslick died August 6, 1904.

Karl Ulrich Schnabel was born August 6, 1909.

Felix Mendelssohn signed the score of his overture, "A Midsummer Night's Dream," on August 6, 1826.

August Seventh

> The soul that becomes discouraged in the presence of real greatness will never become thoroughly artistic. -- Mendelssohn

Alfredo Catalani died August 7, 1893.

Carl Formes was born August 7, 1818.

Sir Granville Bantock was born August 7, 1868.

August Eighth

> Music is the art in which form and matter are always one, the art whose subject cannot be separated from the method of its expression.....the condition to which all the other arts are aspiring. --E. A. Poe

Cecile Chaminade was born August 8, 1857.

Olga Samaroff was born August 8, 1882.

Pietro Yon was born August 8, 1886.

Luigi Marchesi was born August 8, 1754.

August Ninth

> Music is the one incorporeal entrance into the higher
> world of knowledge which comprehends mankind, but
> which mankind cannot comprehend.... Every real crea-
> tion of art is independent, more powerful than the artist
> himself, and returns to the divine through its manifesta-
> tion. --Beethoven

Ruggiero Leoncavallo died August 9, 1919.

American debut of Birgit Nilsson took place on August 9,
1956, at the Hollywood Bowl.

Zino Francescatti was born August 9, 1905.

Berlioz' "Beatrice et Benedict" was first presented on August 9, 1862, at Baden-Baden, with the composer conducting.

Cutner Solomon was born August 9, 1902.

Nicolas Miaskovsky died August 9, 1950.

Ferenc Fricsay was born August 9, 1914.

August Tenth

> A fugue, sonata, or symphony, studied scientifically, in
> all the relations of the separate parts to one another
> and to the whole, demands for its proper comprehension
> intellectual powers and training. --Fillmore

Witold Malcuzynski was born August 10, 1914.

Alexander Glazunov was born August 10, 1865.

Douglas Stuart Moore was born August 10, 1893.

August Eleventh

> Music doth not only expel the greatest griefs, but it
> doth extenuate fears and furies, appeaseth cruelty,
> abateth heaviness, and to such as are watchful it
> causeth great rest. --Cassiodorus

Anton Arensky was born August 11, 1861.

Carrie Jacobs Bond was born August 11, 1862.

The International Society for Contemporary Music was founded August 11, 1922.

Pol Plancon died August 11, 1914.

August Twelfth

> All that is mortal and perishable will gradually weary
> us; truth alone will endure. --Merz

Giovanni Gabrieli died August 12, 1612.

Monument erected to Beethoven at Bonn on August 12, 1845.

Niccolo Amati died August 12, 1684.

Leos Janacek died August 12, 1928.

Maestro Ettore Panizza was born August 12, 1875.

Annibale Pio Fabri, the first truly great tenor, died in Lis-
bon on August 12, 1760.

Franz von Biber was born August 12, 1644.

August Thirteenth

> The air we breathe penetrates even to the inward man.
> A man's life and work are greatly influenced by his
> surroundings. --Schumann

Jules Massenet died August 13, 1912.

Emma Hayden Eames was born August 13, 1865.

John Ireland was born August 13, 1879.

Formal opening of the Bayreuther Festspielhaus with a performance of Wagner's "Der Ring des Nibelungen" on August 13, 1876.

August Fourteenth

> O Music, sphere-descended maid,
> Friend of pleasure, Wisdom's aid!--
>
> Collins

William Croft died August 14, 1727.

Sir Landon Ronald died August 14, 1938.

William Flanagan was born August 14, 1926.

Johann Sebastian Bach assumed the organist post at the Bonifaciuskirche at Arnstadt, Germany, on August 14, 1703.

August Fifteenth

> Perfection even in a sphere the most foreign to us
> leaves its own stamp on the mind. --Mendelssohn

Wanda Landowska died August 15, 1959.

Edwin Hughes was born August 15, 1884.

Emma Calvé was born August 15, 1858.

Joseph Joachim died August 15, 1907.

Rubin Goldmark was born August 15, 1872.

Jacques Ibert was born August 15, 1890.

Julius Katchen was born August 15, 1926.

Lukas Foss was born August 15, 1922.

Gino Marinuzzi died August 15, 1945.

August Sixteenth

> Acquire an early knowledge of directing, watch good
> directors closely and form a habit of directing with
> them silently and to yourself. This brings clearness
> into you.--Schumann

Moura Lympany was born August 16, 1916.

World premiere of Wagner's "Siegfried" took place on August 16, 1876, in Bayreuth.

Sophie Braslau was born August 16, 1892.

August Seventeenth

> Without imagination no perfection in art is possible.--
> Merz

Abram Chasins was born August 17, 1903.

Wagner's "Gotterdammerung" was first performed on August
17, 1876, in Bayreuth. Hans Richter conducted.

Ole Bull, Norwegian violinist, died August 17, 1880.

August Eighteenth

> The teacher is the mediator between the pure and high
> art, as shown in the works of great masters, and be-
> tween the young and the coming generation.--Louis
> Kohler

Friedrich Wieck was born August 18, 1785.

Annette Essipoff died August 18, 1914.

Cosima Liszt and Hans von Bulow were married on August
18, 1857.

Benjamin Godard was born August 18, 1849.

Ludwig Fischer was born August 18, 1745.

Genevieve Ward died August 18, 1922.

August Nineteenth

> Genius, that power which dazzles mortal eyes,
> Is oft but perseverance in disguise. --Henry Austin

Georges Enesco was born August 19, 1881.

Niccolo Porpora, one of the greatest of singing teachers,
was born August 19, 1686.

Serge Diaghilev died August 19, 1929.

Ludwig Wullner was born August 19, 1858.

Sir Henry Wood died August 19, 1944.

August Twentieth

> Consider it a monstrosity to alter or to leave out any-
> thing, or to introduce any new-fangled ornaments, in
> pieces by a good composer. That is the greatest out-
> rage you can do to art. --Schumann

Fanny Bloomfield-Zeisler died August 20, 1927.

Christine Nilsson was born August 20, 1843.

Eric Blom was born August 20, 1888.

Jacopo Peri was born August 20, 1561.

August Twenty-first

> Technique should not seek to shine by itself, and least
> of all give the impression of being the performer's
> strongest point. --Christiani

Hugh Ross was born August 21, 1898.

Paul Juon died August 21, 1940.

Frederick Corder died August 21, 1932.

August Twenty-second

> Art and composition tolerate no conventional fetters;
> mind and soul soar above them. --Joseph Haydn

Claude DeBussy was born August 22, 1862.

Karlheinz Stockhausen was born August 22, 1928.

From Handel's autograph score we learn that the composition
of "Messiah" was begun on the 22nd day of August and completed on the 12th of September in the year 1741, the instrumentation being finished two days later.

Maud Powell was born August 22, 1868.

Vitya Vronsky was born August 22, 1909.

Sofia Scalchi died August 22, 1922.

August Twenty-third

> Music is architecture translated or transposed from
> space into time; for in music, besides the deepest feel-
> ing, there reigns also a rigorous mathematical intelli-
> gence. --Hegel

Moritz Moszkowski was born August 23, 1854.

Teresa Stolz died August 23, 1902.

The Berkshire Symphonic Festival originated in Stockbridge,
Massachusetts, on August 23, 1934.   The founder and conductor was Dr. Henry Hadley.

Albert Roussel died August 23, 1937.

Ernst Krenek was born August 23, 1900.

August Twenty-fourth

> Harmony in music does not consist merely in the con-
> struction of concordant sounds, but in their mutual re-
> lations, their proper succession in what I should call
> their audible reflex. --Delacroix

On August 24, 1960, an audience of more than twelve thou-
sand people heard Maria Callas as Norma in the Greek Am-
phitheater at Epidauros in Greece.   The performance was
directed by the eighty-two year old Tullio Serafin.

Felix Mottl was born August 24, 1856.

Karl Friedrich Curschmann died August 24, 1841.

August Twenty-fifth

> If only the whole world could feel the power of
> harmony.... --Mozart

Richard and Cosima Wagner
entertaining at home.
Painting by W. Beckmann.

First performance of Mozart's Mass in C Minor was presented on August 25, 1783, in Salzburg.

Leonard Bernstein was born August 25, 1918.

Wagner married Liszt's daughter, Cosima, on August 25, 1870.

Joan Sutherland and Nicolai Gedda sang Haydn's "Orfeo ed Euridice" at the Edinburgh Festival on August 25, 1967.

Elizabeth Billington died August 25, 1818.

August Twenty-sixth

> I now feel more vividly than ever what a heavenly art is, and for this also I have to thank my parents. Just when all else which to interest the mind appears so repugnant and empty, the smallest real service to art lays hold of your inmost thoughts, leading you so far away from town and country, and from earth itself, that it is, indeed, a blessing sent by God. --Mendelssohn

First performance of Mendelssohn's oratorio "Elijah" was given on August 26, 1846, in the Birmingham Festival.

Sir Ralph Vaughan-Williams died August 26, 1958.

Umberto Giordano was born August 26, 1867.

Giuseppe de Luca died August 26, 1950.

Mark Hambourg died August 26, 1960.

August Twenty-seventh

> No man loves the country more than I; for do not forests, trees, rocks echo that for which man longs?--Beethoven

Josquin Des Prez, the greatest master of the Renaissance, died August 27, 1521.

Theresa Parodi was born August 27, 1827.

Eric Coates was born August 27, 1886.

Marian Anderson sang with the New York Philharmonic Orchestra on August 27, 1925, after winning a competition over three hundred other contestants.

August Twenty-eighth

> When we speak of grace, enthusiasm, presence of mind, nobility, and warmth of feeling, who does not think of Chopin?--Schumann

Frederic Chopin arrived in Paris on August 28, 1831, and moved into 27 Boulevard Poissoniere.

Richard Tucker was born August 28, 1914.

Premiere performance of Wagner's "Lohengrin" was presented on August 28, 1850, in Weimar, Germany. Franz Liszt conducted the world premiere.

The Marchisio sisters first performed "Semiramide" in Venice on August 28, 1858.

Pergolesis's "La Serva Padrona" was first produced on August 28, 1733, in Naples.

August Twenty-ninth

> You must gradually make acquaintance with all the important works of all the important masters.--Schumann

Emil Paur was born August 29, 1855.

Felicien David died August 29, 1876.

Leonardo De Lorenzo was born August 29, 1875.

First performance given on August 29, 1720, of Handel's oratorio "Esther," dedicated to the Duke of Chandos in England.

Bohuslav Martinu died August 29, 1959.

August Thirtieth

> Books! 'tis a dull and endless strife:
>   Come, hear the woodland linnet,
> How sweet his music! on my life,
>   There's more of wisdom in it. --
>
> Wordsworth

Regina Resnik was born August 30, 1922.

Percy Goetschius was born August 30, 1853.

Gaetano Merola died August 30, 1953.

August Thirty-first

> The man who labors only for money is selfish; he who
> sacrifices all for fame is foolish; he who lives for the
> truth is the true disciple. --Merz

Ramon Vinay was born August 31, 1914.

Francesco Tamagno died August 31, 1905.

Ernest Van Dyck died August 31, 1923.

SEPTEMBER

I pant for music that is divine.--Shelley

September First

There's sure no passion in the human soul,
But finds its food in music.--George Lillo

Amilcare Ponchielli was born September 1, 1834.

Simon Barere was born September 1, 1896.

Engelbert Humperdinck was born September 1, 1854.

Cleofonte Campanini was born September 1, 1860.

Johann Pachelbel was born September 1, 1653.

September Second

Joy is not in things, it is in us!--Wagner

Isidore Philipp was born September 2, 1863.

Friedrich Schorr was born September 2, 1888.

Sydney Beck was born September 2, 1906.

Giulio Gatti-Casazza died September 2, 1940.

Set Svanholm was born September 2, 1904.

September Third

Do not take up the violin unless you mean to work hard
at it. Any other instrument may be more safely trifled
with.--Haweis

Niccolo Amati was born at Cremona on September 3, 1596.

Moriz Rosenthal died September 3, 1946.

The first performance of Schoenberg's "Five Orchestral Pieces" was given on September 3, 1912, at Queen's Hall in London.

Joseph Krips made his conducting debut on September 3, 1921, at the Volksoper in a performance of Verdi's opera "Un Ballo in Maschera."

Eduard Van Beinum was born September 3, 1901.

The Westminster Choir organized on September 3, 1926.

September Fourth

> If an artist does not himself feel what is great, how
> can he succeed in making me feel it?--Mendelssohn

Anton Bruckner was born September 4, 1824.

Edvard Grieg died September 4, 1907.

Albert Schweitzer died September 4, 1965.

Willard Irving Nevins was born September 4, 1890.

Darius Milhaud was born September 4, 1892.

Edoardo Mascheroni was born September 4, 1852.

September Fifth

> Drink of the magical potion music has
>   mixed with her wine,
> Full of the madness of motion, joyful,
>   exultant, divine!--
>
>   Van Dyke

Jacob Meyerbeer was born September 5, 1791.

Louis Kohler was born September 5, 1820.

Rhene-Baton was born September 5, 1879.

Jacob Meyerbeer,
born September 5, 1791.

Marcel Journet died September 5, 1933.

Joseph Szigeti was born September 5, 1892.

Johann Christian Bach was born September 5, 1735.

September Sixth

> Exercise your imagination so that you may acquire the
> power of remembering not only the melody of a compo-
> sition, but also the harmonies which accompany it. --
> Schumann

John Powell was born September 6, 1882.

John Charles Thomas was born September 6, 1891.

Manfred Gurlitt was born September 6, 1890.

Anton Diabelli was born September 6, 1781.

Henry Hadley died September 6, 1937.

September Seventh

> We see that several airs and tunes do please several nations and persons, according to the sympathy they have with their spirits. --Francis Bacon

Jean Louis Duport died September 7, 1819.

Joan Cross was born September 7, 1900.

Julie Dorus-Gras was born September 7, 1805.

Franz Wullner died September 7, 1902.

September Eighth

> Exercise without consciousness is not artistic skill; it is only the working of the instinct, which will always make the want of a complete education sensible. The spiritual thought cannot do without the form, and it is this which must be recognized and learned. --Richter

Antonin Dvorak was born September 8, 1841.

Richard Strauss died September 8, 1949.

Eric Salzman was born September 8, 1933.

September Ninth

> Art is an absolute mistress; she will not be coquetted with or slighted; she requires the most entire self-devotion, and she repays with grand triumphs. --Cushman

Josef Marx was born September 9, 1913.

Jussi Bjorling died September 9, 1960.

September Tenth

> There is no truer truth obtainable
> By man than comes of music. --
>   Robert Browning

Niccolo Jommelli was born September 10, 1714.

Bartolomeo Campagnoli was born September 10, 1751.

Sir George Henschel died September 10, 1934.

World premiere of "Benvenuto Cellini" by Berlioz was given on September 10, 1838, in Paris.

September Eleventh

> Musical criticism, and criticism generally, is, with rare exceptions, no more than the expression of a liking or disliking which has its origin in temperament, habit, and education. --Niecks

Eduard Hanslick, eminent critic and writer, was born September 11, 1825.

Friedrich Kuhlau was born September 11, 1786.

First performance of Stravinsky's opera "The Rake's Progress" was given on September 11, 1951, at the Teatro la Fenice, Venice. Stravinsky conducted the world premiere and the cast included Elisabeth Schwarzkopf and Jennie Tourel.

Robert Schumann presented his wedding gift, the "Liederkreis," song cycle, to Clara Wieck on September 11, 1840, the night before their marriage.

Jenny Lind made her American debut September 11, 1850.

September Twelfth

> That composer is greatest who most clearly discerns the true ends and capabilities of his art; who aims to give worthy expression to the noblest emotional experience. --Fillmore

Robert Schumann and Clara Wieck were married on September 12, 1840 at Schonefeld, near Leipzig.

Marianne Brandt was born September 12, 1842.

Theodore Kullak was born September 12, 1818.

Jean Philip Rameau died September 12, 1764.

Francois Couperin died September 12, 1733.

World premiere performance of Gustav Mahler's Eighth Symphony was given in Munich on September 12, 1910, with the composer conducting.

September Thirteenth

> It is music's lofty mission to shed light on the depths of the human heart. --Schumann

Clara Wieck Schumann was born September 13, 1819.

Arnold Schoenberg was born September 13, 1874.

Julius Rontgen died September 13, 1932.

Emanuel Chabrier died September 13, 1894.

September Fourteenth

> Wheresoever the search after truth begins, there life begins, wheresoever that search ceases, there life ceases. --Ruskin

Luigi Maria Cherubini was born September 14, 1760.

Ossip Gabrilowitsch died September 14, 1936.

Benjamin Cooke died September 14, 1793.

Fritz Busch died September 14, 1951.

September Fifteenth

> Before a man can produce anything great, he must understand the means by which he has to produce it. --Goethe

Anton Webern died September 15, 1945.

Bruno Walter was born September 15, 1876.

Pierre Marie Baillot died September 15, 1842.

Hilde Guden was born September 15, 1917.

September Sixteenth

> Music owes as much to Bach as religion to its founder.
> --<u>Schumann</u>

The Metropolitan gave its first performance in the new house at Lincoln Center on September 16, 1966: world premiere of Samuel Barber's "Antony and Cleopatra."

Nadia Boulanger was born September 16, 1887.

Karol Rathaus was born September 16, 1895.

John McCormack died September 16, 1943.

September Seventeenth

> We cannot understand a complete education of man without music.--<u>Jean Paul Richter</u>

Charles T. Griffes was born September 17, 1884.

September Eighteenth

> Music is the art in which form and matter are always one, the art whose subject cannot be separated from the method of its expression....the condition to which all the other arts are aspiring.--<u>E. A. Poe</u>

Alberto Franchetti was born September 18, 1860.

Arthur Benjamin was born September 18, 1893.

Giuseppina Strepponi was born September 18, 1815.

Frances Alda died September 18, 1952.

September Nineteenth

> Concentrate on legato. Hear great singers. If you want to play the long cantilena in my Scherzo (in B flat

minor), go hear Pasta or Rubini.--<u>Chopin</u>

Gustave Schirmer, Sr. was born September 19, 1829.

First performance of Gustav Mahler's Seventh Symphony was heard September 19, 1908, in Prague, with the composer conducting.

September Twentieth

Music is designed for the masses; it is one of the principal means, outside Christianity, to refine the masses. --<u>Merz</u>

William Kapell was born September 20, 1922.

A notable Rosenkavalier was heard in San Francisco on September 20, 1955, when Elisabeth Schwarzkopf made her American debut.   Erich Leinsdorf conducted.

The 1966 Opera Season in San Francisco opened on September 20 starring Joan Sutherland in Bellini's "I Puritani."

Ildebrando Pizzetti was born September 20, 1880.

September Twenty-first

Passions, however violent, should never be portrayed in all their ugliness; and even when describing the most horrible situations music should never offend, but always remain music.--<u>Mozart</u>

The establishment of the International Mozart Foundation took place on September 21, 1880, in Salzburg.

Gyorgy Sandor was born September 21, 1912.

Johannes Brahms gave his first piano concert September 21, 1848, in Hamburg, Germany.

Gustav Holst was born September 21, 1874.

September Twenty-second

The free arts and the beautiful science of composition will not tolerate technical chains.   The mind and soul must be free.--Haydn

World premiere of Wagner's "Das Rheingold" was given on September 22, 1869, in Munich.   Franz Wullner conducted.

Elisabeth Rethberg was born September 22, 1894.

Julius Stockhausen died September 22, 1906.

September Twenty-third

Melody is the golden thread running through the maze of tones by which the ear is guided and the heart reached. --Christiani

Vincenzo Bellini died on September 23, 1835, at the age of thirty-three, having just completed "I Puritani."

Maria Malibran died September 23, 1836, in Manchester at the age of twenty-eight, having been thrown from a horse.

San Francisco finally heard Joan Sutherland in her most famous role of Lucia on September 23, 1961, when Francesco Molinari-Pradelli conducted.

Gluck's "Armide" was first performed on September 23, 1777, in Paris.

Lincoln Center Day....opening concert at Philharmonic Hall, Lincoln Center, New York City on September 23, 1962, with the New York Philharmonic conducted by Leonard Bernstein, Music Director.

Louis-Gilbert Duprez died September 23, 1896.

Anton Rubinstein gave his first American concert on September 23, 1872, in New York City.

September Twenty-fourth

The fundamental evil in music is the necessity of reproduction of its artistic creations by performance.   Were it as easy to learn to read music as words, the sonatas of Beethoven would have the popularity of the poems of Schiller.--Ferdinand Hiller

Cornell MacNeil was born September 24, 1922.

Ettore Bastianini was born September 24, 1922.

September Twenty-fifth

> It is the duty of every composer to make himself famil-
> iar with all the works of the older and modern poets, in
> order to choose for his vocal music the best and most
> adequate words. --Beethoven

Dimitri Shostakovitch was born September 25, 1906.

Johann Strauss (the Elder) died September 25, 1849.

Glen Gould was born September 25, 1932.

Jean Philip Rameau was born September 25, 1683.

Gerda Lammers was born September 25, 1915.

September Twenty-sixth

> True art is the result of knowledge and inspiration. --
> Berlioz

The first performance of Donizetti's "Lucia di Lammermoor"
was given at the Teatro San Carlos in Naples on September
26, 1835.   Lucia was an immediate triumph.   Fanny Persiani was the first Lucia.

George Gershwin was born September 26, 1898.

Charles Munch was born September 26, 1891.

Bela Bartok died September 26, 1945.

Alfred Cortot was born September 26, 1877.

Sylvia Marlowe was born September 26, 1908.

"Lucia di Lammermoor,"
first performed in Naples
on September 26, 1835.

September Twenty-seventh

All inmost things, we may say, are melodius, naturally
utter themselves in song. The meaning of song goes
deep. Who is there that, in logical words, can express
the effect music has on us?--Carlyle

Adelina Patti died September 27, 1919.

Elly Ney was born September 27, 1882.

Cyril Scott was born September 27, 1879.

Engelbert Humperdinck died September 27, 1921.

September Twenty-eighth

Music is a discipline, and a mistress of order and
good manners.--Martin Luther

Florent Schmitt was born September 28, 1870.

Stravinsky's "Histoire du Soldat" was first performed on September 28, 1918, in Lausanne.

Charles Lamoureux was born September 28, 1834.

September Twenty-ninth

> A truly inspired artist always plunges into his work with enthusiastic abandon. --Wagner

Richard Bonynge was born September 29, 1930.

The opera debut of Emma Calvé took place on September 29, 1882, in "Faust" at the Theatre de la Monnaie in Brussels.

Franco Capuana was born September 29, 1894.

Leopoldo Mugnone was born September 29, 1858.

Rosa Raisa died September 29, 1963.

September Thirtieth

> We live in this world in order always to learn industriously, and to enlighten each other by means of discussion, and to strive vigorously to promote the progress of science and the fine arts. --Mozart

Mozart conducted the opening performance of "Die Zauberflöte" on September 30, 1791, in Vienna.

David Oistrakh was born September 30, 1908.

"Porgy and Bess" was first performed on September 30, 1935, in Boston.

They ar...
by nob...

October First

> Touch is to the pianist ... a good management of the
> voice is to the vocalist, o... good action of the bow to
> a violinist--the means of produ... ... ...able sounds
> and of executing difficulties. --Taylor

Vladimir Horowitz was born October 1, 1904.

Benno Moiseiwitsch made his concert debut on October 1,
1908, in England.

Ernst von Dohnanyi made his debut as a concert pianist on
October 1, 1897, in Berlin.

Paul Dukas was born October 1, 1865.

On October 1, 1811, Napoleon sat through a private performance of "Cosi fan tutti" at Compiegne.

The Curtis Institute of Music in Philadelphia was inaugurated
on October 1, 1924.

Henry Bertini died October 1, 1876.

John Blow died October 1, 1708.

Pierre Marie Baillot was born October 1, 1771.

October Second

> In my opinion a musician's real work only begins when
> he has reached what is called perfection, viz., a point
> beyond which he has nothing apparently to learn. --
> Mendelssohn

Franz Liszt was appointed Court Kappelmeister at Weimar

on October 2, 1842.

A mass in honor of Bellini was held on October 2, 1835.
A Requiem by Cherubini was sung, and a Lacrymosa from
the "Credeasi misera" in the last act of Puritani was sung
by Rubini, Ivanov, Tamburini and Lablache.

Max Bruch died October 2, 1920.

Henri Fevrier was born October 2, 1875.

The Academy of Music in New York was inaugurated on October 2, 1854.

October Third

> The man that hath no music in himself
> Nor is not mov'd with concord of sweet sounds,
> Is fit for treasons, stratagems, and spoils.
> The motions of his spirit are dull as night,
> And his affections dark as Erebus;
>   Let no such man be trusted. --
>   Shakespeare

"The Dream of Gerontius," generally acclaimed as Elgar's
masterpiece, was first performed October 3, 1900, at the
Birmingham Festival, under the direction of Hans Richter.

The New York City Opera was inaugurated on October 3,
1944.

Maestro Stanislaw Skrowaczewski was born October 3, 1923.

Therese Tietjens died October 3, 1877.

Wilhelm Kienzl died October 3, 1941.

Sir Arnold Bax died October 3, 1953.

Sir Malcolm Sargent died October 3, 1967.

Carl Nielsen died October 3, 1931.

October Fourth

> Is not the precept of a musician to fall from a discord
> or harsh accord alike true in affection? Is not the de-
> light of quavering upon a stop in music the same with
> the playing of light upon the water?--Bacon

Fanny Persiani was born October 4, 1812.

Jaques Offenbach died October 4, 1880.

Set Svanholm died October 4, 1964.

Louis Duport was born October 4, 1749.

Giovanni Battista ("Padre") Martini died October 4, 1784.

October Fifth

> We are often made to feel with a shivering delight that
> from an earthly harp are stricken notes which cannot
> have been unfamiliar to the angels.--Edgar Allan Poe

The first performance of Gluck's opera "Orpheo ed Eurydice"
was given on October 5, 1762, in Vienna.

Alfred V. Frankenstein was born October 5, 1906.

October Sixth

> Jenny Lind sang Mendelssohn's 'Hear My Prayer' so
> exquisitely that none who heard it can ever forget the
> impression she created.--Moscheles

Jenny Lind was born October 6, 1820.

On October 6, 1920, Frieda Hempel gave the first of her
Jenny Lind Concerts in honor of the centenary of the birth
of that singer.

Paul Baduro-Skoda was born October 6, 1927.

The first performance of Jacopo Peri's opera "Euridice,"
the earliest opera of which the music has survived, and
composed for the wedding of Henry IV of France and Marie

di Medici, was first performed on October 6, 1600, in Florence.

Maria Jeritza was born October 6, 1887.

Edwin Fischer was born October 6, 1886.

October Seventh

> A critic is justified in seeking and pronouncing the truth without reserve. It is not his duty to consider whom he pleases or offends by his candor. --Ambros

Frieda Hempel died October 7, 1955.

American debut of Ilma di Murska was on October 7, 1873, at the Grand Opera House of New York.

The London Philharmonic gave its first concert on October 7, 1932, with Sir Thomas Beecham conducting.

World premiere of "Le Coq d'Or" by Rimsky-Korsakov took place October 7, 1909, in Moscow.

Isabella Colbran died October 7, 1845.

Alfred Wallenstein was born October 7, 1898.

October Eighth

> Sing aloud old songs....the precious music of the heart. --Wordsworth

Irene Dalis was born October 8, 1925.

Emil von Sauer was born October 8, 1862.

The Bergen Symphony Orchestra in Norway was founded on October 8, 1765.

Heinrich Ernst died October 8, 1865.

The first issue of "Musical America" was published on October 8, 1898.

October Ninth

> Music is a kind of inarticulate unfathomable speech,
> which leads us to the edge of the infinite, and lets us
> for moments gaze into that. --Carlyle

Camille Saint-Saens was born October 9, 1835.

Gunther Schuller's "The Trial" was given its premiere by
Hamburg State Opera on October 9, 1966.

October Tenth

> All that is good in art is the expression of one soul
> talking to another, and is precious according to the
> greatness of the soul that utters it. --Ruskin

Giuseppe Verdi was born October 10, 1813.

Giuseppe Verdi,
born October 10, 1813.

World premiere of Strauss' "Die Frau Ohne Schatten" was given on October 10, 1919, at the Vienna Opera. Franz Schalk conducted and the cast included Maria Jeritza and Lotte Lehmann.

Alexander Siloti was born October 10, 1863.

Paul Creston was born October 10, 1906.

Vaughan-Williams' "A Sea Symphony" was first performed on October 10, 1910, at Leeds.

October Eleventh

> I knew of only one who may be compared to Beethoven, and he is Bruckner. --Wagner

Anton Bruckner died October 11, 1896.

Piano Concerto No. 1 by Frederic Chopin was heard for the first time on October 11, 1830, in Warsaw, with the composer as soloist.

Leopold Stokowski gave his first concert in Philadelphia on October 11, 1912.

Isaac Stern made his New York debut on October 11, 1937.

October Twelfth

> The barriers are not erected that can say to aspiring talents and industry, 'Thus far and no further.'--Beethoven

Ralph Vaughan-Williams was born October 12, 1872.

"Lucia di Lammermoor" was presented at the Metropolitan Opera House with Joan Sutherland on October 12, 1964, under the direction of Silvio Varviso.

Alwina Valleria, first American to sing at the Metropolitan Opera, was born on October 12, 1848.

Gala world premiere of Gunther Schuller's "The Visitation" was presented on October 12, 1966, at the Hamburg Opera Festival.

October Thirteenth

> Merely to have learned how to learn is a great advance.
> --Menander

Nellie Melba, after less than a year of study, made her operatic debut as Gilda at the Theatre de la Monnaie in Brussels on October 13, 1887.

Moritz Hauptmann was born October 13, 1792.

Peter van Anrooy was born October 13, 1879.

Gosta Nystroem was born October 13, 1890.

October Fourteenth

> A tempo is correct when everything can still be heard. When a figure can no longer be understood because the tones run into one another, then the tempo is too fast. In a Presto the extreme limit of distinctness is the correct tempo, beyond this it loses its effectiveness. -- Mahler

The first performance of Rachmaninoff's Piano Concerto No. 2 in C Minor was given in Moscow on October 14, 1901, with the composer at the piano. It has become Rachmaninoff's best-loved orchestral work.

Mischa Elman made his bow in Berlin on October 14, 1904. He was twelve years old.

Gary Graffman was born October 14, 1928.

Paul Chevillard was born October 14, 1859.

October Fifteenth

> Think more of your own progress than of the opinion of others. --Mendelssohn

Antonio Cotogni, Italy's greatest baritone of all time, died October 15, 1918. He was also that rarity: a great singer who becomes a great teacher.

Geraldine Farrar made her debut in Grand Opera October 15, 1901, in Gounod's "Faust" in Berlin. She was nineteen years old.

"La Mer" by Claude DeBussy was first performed October 15, 1905, in Paris under the direction of Paul Chevillard.

Wieland Wagner died October 15, 1966.

Madame Caradori-Allan died October 15, 1865.

October Sixteenth

> The belief in technique as the only means of salvation must be suppressed, the striving toward truth furthered. --Arnold Schoenberg

Schoenberg's "Pierrot Lunaire" was first performed on October 16, 1912, in Berlin.

Teresa Stratas made her operatic debut on October 16, 1958, at the Toronto Opera Festival.

Maurice Renaud died October 16, 1933.

Sir Granville Bantock died October 16, 1946.

October Seventeenth

> In every piece we find, in his own refined hand, written in pearls: 'This is by Frederic Chopin.' We recognize him even in his pauses, and by his impetuous respiration. He is the boldest, the proudest poet soul of today. --Schumann

Frederic Chopin died October 17, 1849.

American debut of Mischa Levitzki at Aeolian Hall in New York on October 17, 1916.

Johann Nepomuk Hummel died October 17, 1837.

Giovanni Matteo Mario, tenor, was born October 17, 1810.

He married the soprano Giulia Grisi.

The death of Chopin--
from painting by Felix Joseph Barrias.

Johann Sebastian Bach married Marie Barbara Bach, his cousin, on October 17, 1707.

October Eighteenth

Music is the sound of universal laws promulgated. -- Thoreau

Charles Francois Gounod died October 18, 1893.

Etienne Henri Mehul died October 18, 1817.

The La Scala Opera Company made its American debut at Carnegie Hall, New York, on October 18, 1967, in Verdi's "Requiem."

October Nineteenth

> You should no more play without phrasing than speak
> without inflection and grammatical pauses. --Landon

Emil Gilels was born October 19, 1916.

The first performance of Rameau's opera "Dardanus" was
presented on October 19, 1739, in Paris.

Wagner's "Tannhauser" was first performed on October 19,
1845, in Dresden. The cast included Johanna Wagner, Wilhelmine Schroder-Devrient and Joseph Aloys Tichatschek.

October Twentieth

> Although woman has never made an epoch in musical
> art, it must be said that she has done a very important
> work in its development. Though she has never been a
> great composer, she has surely been great in the inter-
> pretation of art-works. --Anon.

On October 20, 1960, Joan Sutherland gave a spell-binding
performance at Covent Garden as Anima in "La Sonnambula."

Adelina Patti made her last public appearance on October
20, 1914, in Albert Hall.

The opening night for "Rienza" was on October 20, 1842, in
Dresden, giving Richard Wagner his first taste of popular
favor.

Alfred Cortot appeared in America for the first time on Oc-
tober 20, 1918, when he appeared as soloist with the visiting
French Symphony Orchestra playing the Saint-Saens Fourth
Piano Concerto under the direction of Andre Messager.

Michael William Balfe died October 20, 1870.

Lilli Lehmann made her operatic debut in Prague on October
20, 1865, a month before her seventeenth birthday. She appeared as the First Boy in "The Magic Flute."

Charles Edward Ives was born October 20, 1874.

October Twenty-first

Harmony is a beautiful problem of which melody is the solution. --Gretry

George Solti was born October 21, 1912.

Julius Katchen made his debut with the Philadelphia Orchestra on October 21, 1937.

Offenbach's "Orphee aux Enfers" was heard for the first time on October 21, 1858, in Paris.

October Twenty-second

Music is at once a sentiment and a science; it demands of him who cultivates it, be he executant or composer, natural inspiration and a knowledge which is only to be acquired by protracted studies and profound meditations. --Berlioz

Franz Liszt was born October 22, 1811.

The Metropolitan Opera House was inaugurated on October 22, 1883, with a performance of Gounod's "Faust." The cast included Christine Nilsson, Italo Campanini, Sofia Scalchi and Giuseppe Del Puente.

Giovanni Martinelli was born October 22, 1885.

Leopold Damrosch was born October 22, 1832.

Frank La Forge was born October 22, 1879.

The first concert given by the Boston Symphony Orchestra was on October 22, 1881.

Ludwig Spohr died October 22, 1859.

Victor Maurel died October 22, 1923.

October Twenty-third

You may be a genius and still trample art underfoot. You may be one only possessing meager talent and still

claim the respect due to him who strives worthily. --
Ferdinand von Hiller

Jean Absil, one of the founders of the "Revve Internationale
De Musique," was born October 23, 1893.

Gustav Albert Lortzing was born October 23, 1801.

October Twenty-fourth

To the true artist music should be a necessity, not
merely an occupation.   He should not manufacture
music; he should live in it. --Robert Franz

Alessandro Scarlatti died October 24, 1725.

Florence Easton was born October 24, 1884.

Franz Lehar died October 24, 1948.

Marcello Sembrich made her American debut in "Lucia di
Lammermoor" on October 24, 1883, at the Metropolitan
Opera in New York.

Tito Gobbi was born October 24, 1915.

The first concert of the Los Angeles Philharmonic Orchestra
was given on October 24, 1919.

Victorio De Los Angeles made her American debut at Carnegie Hall, New York on October 24, 1950, joining the Metropolitan Opera that year.

Ferdinand Hiller was born October 24, 1811.

Franco Leoni was born October 24, 1864.

October Twenty-fifth

I hold that every composer has a merit of his own
which is determined by the intrinsic value of his works.
--C. P. E. Bach

Alexandre Georges Bizet was born October 25, 1838.

Tchaikowsky's First Piano Concerto had its world premiere in Boston where it was played by Hans von Bulow on October 25, 1875.

Johann Strauss (the Younger), the "Waltz King," was born October 25, 1825.

The Fourth Symphony of Johannes Brahms was heard for the first time on October 25, 1885, in Meiningen, with the composer conducting.

World premiere of Weber's "Euryanthe" was presented on October 25, 1823, in Vienna. Henrietta Sontag had the name role.

The inauguration of Steinway Hall in New York took place October 25, 1925.

October Twenty-sixth

> Dare talent permit itself to take the same liberties as genius? Yes; but the former will perish where the latter triumphs. --Robert Schumann

Domenico Scarlatti was born October 26, 1685.

Walter Gieseking died October 26, 1956.

The Second Symphony of Bruckner, dedicated to Franz Liszt, was first performed on October 26, 1873, in Vienna, with the composer conducting.

Metropolitan premiere of Verdi's "Il Trovatore" was presented on October 26, 1883. The cast included Alwina Valleria, Zelia Trebelli and Giuseppe Kaschmann.

October Twenty-seventh

> Paganini is one of those artists of whom it must be said: 'They are because they are and not because others were before them.'--Berlioz

Niccolo Paganini was born October 27, 1782.

Jasha Heifetz made his American debut at Carnegie Hall, New York, on October 27, 1917.

Christine Nilsson made her debut at the Theatre Lyrique in Paris on October 27, 1864, as Violetta in "La Traviata."

World premiere of Bellini's "Il Pirata" was given on October 27, 1827, at La Scala in Milan. The original cast included Henriette-Clementine Meric-Lalande, Giovanni-Battista Rubini and Antonio Tamburini.

October Twenty-eighth

> Musical training is a more potent instrument than any other, because rhythm and harmony find their way into the inward places of the soul. --Plato

Tchaikowsky conducted the premiere of his Symphony Pathetique on October 28, 1893, in St. Petersburg.

Caroline Unger, for whom Donizetti wrote "Parisina," was born October 28, 1803. Franz Liszt admired her immensely as artist and woman.

Howard Hanson was born October 28, 1896.

American premiere of Gunther Schuller's opera "The Visitation" was presented on October 28, 1967, in San Francisco, with the composer conducting.

Gasparo Pacchierotti, famous male soprano who sang at the opening of La Scala in 1778, died on October 28, 1821.

Claramae Turner was born October 28, 1920.

Metropolitan debut of Teresa Stratas took place on October 28, 1959.

Henri Bertini was born October 28, 1798.

October Twenty-ninth

> Music is God's best gift to man, the only art of heaven given to earth, the only art of earth we take to heaven. --Landor

Maria Callas made a spectacular first appearance with the Metropolitan Opera on October 29, 1956, singing Bellini's "Norma." Fausta Cleva conducted

William Kapell was killed in a plane crash near San Francisco on October 29, 1953.

Gina Bachauer's New York debut took place on October 29, 1950.

World premiere of Mozart's opera "Don Giovanni" was given on October 29, 1787, in Prague.

Jon Vickers was born October 29, 1926.

Byron Janis made his New York debut with a recital at Carnegie Hall on October 29, 1948.

October Thirtieth

> Playing notes right is not enough.   Mere technical virtuosity is not enough.   Music must speak--or it is nothing. --Leschetizky

Ethel Newcomb was born October 30, 1875.

Peter Warlock was born October 30, 1894.

New work by Darius Milhaud, "Music for Indiana," was performed on October 30, 1966, by the Indianapolis Symphony.

October Thirty-first

> An artist should never lose sight of the thing as a whole. He who puts too much into details will find that the thread which holds the whole thing together will break. --F. Chopin

Saint-Saens' Piano Concerto No. 4 was first performed October 31, 1875, at a Colonne concert in the Chatelet Theatre, Paris, with the composer as soloist.

Operatic debut of Lucrezia Bori took place October 31, 1908, in Rome.

Nicolas Medtner first appeared in America as soloist with the Philadelphia Orchestra in his First Piano Concerto on October 31, 1924.

Julie Rive-King was born October 31, 1857.

Metropolitan premiere of "Mignon" was presented October 31, 1883, with Christine Nilsson, Victor Capoul, Sofia Scalchi and Giuseppe del Puente.

Professor Max Pauer was born October 31, 1866.

Last public appearance of Dame Myra Hess was at Festival Hall, London, on October 31, 1961, when she played the Mozart A Major Concerto under Sir Adrian Boult.

"Mignon," first presented at the
Metropolitan on October 31, 1883.

NOVEMBER

All deep things are song. --Carlyle

November First

> The cultivated musician may study a Madonna by Raphael,
> the painter a symphony by Mozart, with equal advantage.
> Yet more: in sculpture, the actor's art becomes fixed;
> the actor in turn transforms the sculptor's work into liv-
> ing forms; the painter turns a poem into a painting; the
> musician sets a picture to music. --Schumann

The unforgettable American debut of Maria Callas took place
in Chicago on November 1, 1954, in "Norma."

Victoria de Los Angeles was born November 1, 1923.

Sviatoslov Richter made his American debut on November 1,
1960, at Symphony Hall in Boston.

Frederic Chopin left Poland on November 1, 1830, never
again to return to his homeland.

Metropolitan debut of Ezio Pinza was on November 1, 1926,
in "La Vestale."

Alexander Lambert was born November 1, 1863.

Max Trapp was born November 1, 1887.

American debut of Anja Silja took place November 1, 1968,
in San Francisco when she appeared in the all new Wieland
Wagner version of Strauss' "Salome." Wieland Wagner
created the role especially for Miss Silja.

November Second

> Jenny Lind's true spell consisted, in my opinion, in
> these things: in the perfection of her technical culture--

perfection to an extent that caused the most finished
art to appear the most finished nature. --Elise Polko

Jenny Lind died November 2, 1887.

Brahms' "Variations on a Theme by Haydn" was introduced
on November 2, 1873, in Vienna.

Dimitri Mitropoulos died November 2, 1960.

Sir Thomas Beecham gave his first London concert November 2, 1907.

Luisa Tetrazzini made her London debut as Violetta in "La
Traviata" at Covent Garden on November 2, 1907.

Clara Louise Kellogg sang Marguerite in the New York premiere of "Faust" on November 2, 1867.

Auguste Vianesi was born November 2, 1837.

November Third

From Bellini one may learn what melody is. --Wagner

Vincenzo Bellini was born November 3, 1801.

Maestro Tullio Serafin made his American debut at the Metropolitan Opera on November 3, 1924, the opera being
"Aida."

November 3, 1836: Mendelssohn played Beethoven's "G
Major Concerto" to-day with a perfection and power that
carried everything before it. --(From Henrietta Voight's
Diary)

November Fourth

It is a charming test of Mendelssohn's heart that all the
friendships he ever formed endured to the end of his
life. --Elise Polko

Felix Mendelssohn-Barthody died November 4, 1847.

Karl Tausig was born November 4, 1841.

Brahms' First Symphony was heard for the first time on November 4, 1876, at Carlsruhe under the direction of Otto Dessoff.

Gabriel Faure died November 4, 1924.

Toscanini's conducting debut in Italy took place on November 4, 1886, in Turin in the performance of a modern work, Alfredo Catalini's "Edmea."

Faustina Bordoni, one of the first prima donnas to achieve international fame, died November 4, 1781.

World premiere of the Symphonique Poem "Finlandia" by Sibelius was presented on November 4, 1899.

American debut of Titta Ruffo took place on November 4, 1912. He created a sensation!

The San Carlo Opera House in Naples was inaugurated on November 4, 1737.

World premiere of Borodin's "Prince Igor" was produced in St. Petersburg on November 4, 1890.

Sergei Rachmaninoff made his American debut as a pianist on November 4, 1909, at Smith College in Northampton, Massachusetts.

Leon Fleisher played with the New York Philharmonic Orchestra on November 4, 1944, under the baton of Pierre Monteux. This was Fleisher's New York bow.

November Fifth

> The musician cannot transcribe Nature, but he can tell us what he felt at her touch. --Barbedetti

Walter Gieseking was born November 5, 1895.

Paul Wittgenstein was born November 5, 1887.

Erminia Frezzolini, one of the greatest sopranos of all time, died November 5, 1884. Verdi wrote: "Of all the many singers I have heard, I hold dearest in Memory for their greatness Frezzolini and Moriani (tenor)."

Hans Sachs was born November 5, 1494, at Nuremberg.

First performance of Schumann's Second Symphony in C
Major was given November 5, 1846, in Leipzig.

November Sixth

> Paderewski is an artist by the grace of God, a phenom-
> enal and inspired player. --William Mason

Ignaz Paderewski was born November 6, 1860.

Ignaz Paderewski,
"a phenomenal and inspired player, "
born November 6, 1860.

Peter Ilyitch Tchaikovsky died November 6, 1893.

Rachmaninoff's "Rhapsody on a Theme of Paganini" for piano
and orchestra was first introduced on November 7, 1934, by
the Philadelphia Orchestra, with Stokowski conducting and
Rachmaninoff playing the piano part.

Cesare Siepi's Metropolitan debut took place on November 6, 1950, in "Don Carlos."

John Philip Sousa was born November 6, 1854.

Sigismond Stojowski died November 6, 1946.

Marietta Brambilla died November 6, 1875.

Bartolommeo Campagnoli died November 6, 1827.

Paul Kalisch was born November 6, 1855.

Charles Munch died November 6, 1968.

November Seventh

> Then give us the artist whose selfless devotion
> To Art and her service is earnest and true,
> To read us the mystical meaning of music;
> Musicians are many, but artists are few. --
> Perry

Joan Sutherland was born November 7, 1926.

Efram Kurtz was born November 7, 1900.

Max Alvary died November 7, 1898.

Hermann Levi was born November 7, 1839.

November Eighth

> The aim of all the arts is the same, though every one
> of them arrives at its own ends by different roads. --
> Ritter

Cesar Franck died November 8, 1890.

Sir Arnold Bax was born November 8, 1883.

Maria Callas made her first appearance at London's Covent Garden on November 8, 1952. She sang "Norma."

New York premiere of "Hérodiade" took place on November 8,

1909, with Lina Cavalieri as Herodias.

Alberto Erede was born November 8, 1908.

November Ninth

> The most talented composers of the present day are
> pianists--a fact that has been observed during former
> epochs.--Schumann

Brahms' Second Piano Concerto in B Flat Major was first
heard on November 9, 1881, in Budapest, with the composer
at the piano.

Fritz Kreisler's American debut took place on November 9,
1888, in Boston.

Moriz Rosenthal made his first appearance in America on
November 9, 1888, in Boston.

Metropolitan premiere of "Siegfried" was presented November 9, 1887, with Anton Seidl conducting. The stars of the
first New York performance: Emil Fischer, Max Alvary,
Lilli Lehmann and Marianne Brandt.

Hindemith's "Cardillac" was first produced on November 9,
1926, in Dresden. Fritz Busch conducted.

Antonio Tamburini died November 9, 1876.

November Tenth

> Every difficulty slurred over will be a ghost to disturb
> your repose later on.--Chopin

World premiere of "Zaza" was given on November 10, 1900,
at the Teatro Lirico in Milan. Rosina Storchio had the name
role.

John McCormack made his debut November 10, 1909, appearing as Alfredo in "La Traviata."

Francois Couperin was born November 10, 1668.

"La Forza del Destino" was composed to order for the Im-

perial Opera, St. Petersburg, and its reception there, on
November 10, 1862, won Verdi a decoration from Alexander
II.

November Eleventh

> The artist never seeks to represent the positive truth,
> but the idealized image of the truth.--Bulwer

The American debut of Lucrezia Bori at the Metropolitan
Opera took place on November 11, 1912, in "Manon Lescaut"
with Enrico Caruso as Des Grieux.

Alexander Borodin was born November 11, 1833.

Eleanor Spencer played for the first time in America on
November 11, 1913, at Carnegie Hall in New York.

World premiere of Richard Strauss' tone poem "Don Juan"
was given on November 11, 1889, at Weimar.

Sir Thomas Beecham conducted his first adult concert on
November 11, 1899, in Huyton.

Auguste Vianesi died November 11, 1908.

Ernest Ansermet was born November 11, 1883.

November Twelfth

> True genius, so far from imitating the productions of
> others which command its admiration, is only impelled
> to new efforts by them.--Weber

Umberto Giordana died November 12, 1948.

The Metropolitan premiere of "Aida" took place on November 12, 1886, with Anton Seidl conducting.

American debut of Ossip Gabrilowitch was given on November 12, 1900, at Carnegie Hall, New York.

November Thirteenth

> In the abstract we may regard melody as the moving
> element; harmony, on the other hand, as the stable ele-

ment in music.--Hauptmann

Gioacchino Rossini died November 13, 1868.

George London made his Metropolitan debut as Amonasro in "Aida" on November 13, 1951.

Nicolas Medtner died November 13, 1951.

Carlo Bergonzi made his Metropolitan debut as Radames in "Aida" on November 13, 1956.

George Whitefield Chadwick was born November 13, 1854.

Mu Phi Epsilon, National Music Honor Sorority, was founded at the Metropolitan College of Music, Cincinnati, on November 13, 1903.

November Fourteenth

An assiduous and persevering cultivation of a talent is as necessary as the talent itself.--Engel

Theodor Leschetizky died November 14, 1915.

Leopold Mozart was born November 14, 1719.

Leonard Bernstein made his official conducting debut on November 14, 1943, when he appeared with the New York Philharmonic as a last-minute substitute for Bruno Walter.

Yehudi Menuhin appeared in Leipzig, November 14, 1931, on the occasion of the 150th Anniversary of the founding of the Gwendhaus Orchestra, playing the Mendelssohn Concerto.

Metropolitan debut of Amelita Galli-Curci as Violetta in "La Traviata" took place November 14, 1921.

Fanny Cecile Mendelssohn was born November 14, 1805.

Ravel's "Bolero" created a sensation in New York when first performed there by Arturo Toscanini and the New York Philharmonic on November 14, 1929.

Manuel de Falla died November 14, 1946.

Aaron Copland was born November 14, 1900.

Johann Nepomuk Hummel was born November 14, 1778.

American premiere of "Armide" took place on November 14, 1910, with Enrico Caruso, Olive Fremstad, Louise Homer, and with Toscanini conducting.

Anna Moffa made her bow at the Metropolitan in "La Traviata" on November 14, 1959.

Gasparo Luigi Spontini was born November 14, 1774.

Giuseppina Strepponi died November 14, 1897.

Italo Campanini died November 14, 1896.

Jean Madeira was born November 14, 1924.

Metropolitan premiere of "La Sonnambula" took place November 14, 1883. The cast included Marcella Sembrich and Italo Campanini. Cleofonte Campanini, Italo's younger brother, conducted.

November Fifteenth

> The operas of Gluck can only be studied as they deserve by being heard and seen, and, moreover, under conditions of careful and magnificent presentation. --Chorley

Christoph W. Gluck died November 15, 1787.

Beethoven's Fourth Symphony was heard for the first time on November 15, 1807.

Myra Hess made her debut at Queen's Hall on November 15, 1907, playing Beethoven's Concerto in G with Sir Thomas Beecham conducting.

Rosa Ponselle made her debut at the age of twenty-one in "Le Forza del Destino" at the Metropolitan Opera on November 15, 1918.

Enrico Caruso's last opening night at the Metropolitan was on November 15, 1920, in "La Juive."

Guiomar Novaes made her bow in America on November 15, 1915, in New York.

Fritz Reiner died November 15, 1963, in New York.

Metropolitan debut of Gladys Swarthout as La Cieca in "La Gioconda" took place on November 15, 1929.

Jorge Bolet was born November 15, 1914.

Jeanette Scovotti made her Metropolitan Opera debut on November 15, 1962.

November Sixteenth

>   Music, whatever sound and structure it may assume, remains meaningless noise unless it touches a receiving mind. --Hindemith

Paul Hindemith was born November 16, 1895.

Enrico Caruso made his official debut November 16, 1894, in Naples.

Joan Sutherland made her American debut on November 16, 1960, in Handel's "Alcina" at Dallas, Texas.

American debut of Arturo Toscanini and Emma Destinn took place November 16, 1908, at the Metropolitan Opera in "Aida."

Lawrence Tibbett was born November 16, 1896.

The first concert given by the Philadelphia Orchestra was on November 16, 1900.

Metropolitan premiere of "Rigoletto" took place November 16, 1883. The cast included Marcella Sembrich and Sofia Scalchi.

Minnie Hauk was born November 16, 1852.

American premiere of "Turandot" took place at the Metropolitan Opera on November 16, 1926, with Tullio Serafin conducting. The cast included Maria Jeritza, Giacomo Lauri-Volpi and Giuseppe De Luca.

On November 16, 1848, a Polish ball and concert were given in London and Chopin volunteered his services for the occasion. It was destined to be his last appearance in public.

November Seventeenth

> As you ascend the mountain, the horizon expands, and
> your eye will there be able to behold scenes, which were
> shut out from your view before.   Thus it is with the en-
> joyment of music. --Merz

The first New York appearance of Paderewski occurred on
November 17, 1891, at Carnegie Hall.

Roberta Peters' opera debut took place at the Metropolitan
Opera as Zerlina in "Don Giovanni" on November 17, 1950.

Tchaikowsky's Fifth Symphony was first performed on November 17, 1888, in St. Petersburg.

Ernestine Schumann-Heink died November 17, 1936.

Verdi's first opera "Oberto" was given its world premiere at
the Milan Theatre November 17, 1839.   The Leonora of the
first cast was Giuseppina Strepponi, who twenty years later
became Verdi's second wife.

Mathilda Marchisi died November 17, 1913.

World premiere of "Mignon" was presented November 17,
1866, in Paris.   Marie-Celestine Galli-Marie was the first
Mignon.

August Wilhelm Ambros was born November 17, 1816.

The first appearance of Pierre Monteux with the Metropolitan
Opera was on November 17, 1917, the opera being "Faust"
with Geraldine Farrar, Giovanni Martinelli and Leon Rothier.

David Amram was born November 17, 1930.

Metropolitan premiere performance of "Tannhauser" was presented on November 17, 1884.   Leopold Damrosch conducted.

"Fedora" (Giordano) was heard for the first time on November 17, 1898, in Milan.   Enrico Caruso participated in the
world premiere which was conducted by the composer.

Heitor Villa-Lobos died November 17, 1959.

November Eighteenth

> However so-called sober-minded musicians may dispar-
> age consummate brilliancy, it is none the less true that
> every genuine artist has an instinctive desire for it. --
> Liszt

Carl Maria von Weber was born November 18, 1786.

Amelita Galli-Curci was born November 18, 1882.

Eugene Ormandy was born November 18, 1899.

Pauline Viardot-Garcia's triumphal appearance as Orpheus
at the Theatre Lyrique was on November 18, 1859.

Metropolitan premiere of "Adriana Lecouvreur" was given on
November 18, 1907, with Lina Cavalieri in the title role,
Caruso as Maurizio, and Antonio Scotti as Michonnet.

November Nineteenth

> Schubert's songs: Beautiful as are his symphonies, and
> great as was the treasure he bequeathed to the world in
> his instrumental works, his most important contribution
> to musical progress is to be found in his songs, of
> which he wrote some six hundred. --Fillmore

Franz Peter Schubert died November 19, 1828.

The New York debut of Alexander Brailowsky took place on
November 19, 1924, at Aeolian Hall.

Geraldine Farrar made her New York debut as Carmen on
November 19, 1914, with Toscanini conducting and with a
spectacular cast including Caruso.

The first Metropolitan Lenora (Fidelio) was Marianne Brandt,
who made it her New York debut role on November 19, 1884.
Leopold Damrosch conducted.

Anda Geza was born November 19, 1921.

Michael Ippolitoff-Ivanoff was born November 19, 1859.

Franz Schubert in Hungary,
taking notes on the music
played by a gypsy band.

November Twentieth

Rubinstein occupies a unique position among all his con-
temporaries. As a pianist he holds perhaps the first
place since Liszt's death. At the same time, as a composer, not alone for the piano, but in a more marked
degree as a writer of large works, he has made an ex-
traordinary success. --Upton

Anton Rubinstein died November 20, 1894.

Beethoven's "Fidelio" was first performed on November 20,
1805, in Vienna. Beethoven conducted the premiere. The
Leonore was a nineteen year old girl named Anna Milder.

David Oistrakh made his American debut November 20, 1955,
in Carnegie Hall.

The Metropolitan debut of Beniamino Gigli in "Mefistofele"

was presented on November 20, 1920. In the cast with him were Frances Alda, Florence Easton and Adamo Didur.

The debut of Giovanni Martinelli as Rodolfo in "La Boheme" took place on November 20, 1913.

Mahler's "Das Lied von der Erde" was first performed November 20, 1911, in Munich.

Elisabeth Schumann first appeared at the Metropolitan Opera on November 20, 1914, in "Der Rosenkavalier."

Friedrich Himmel was born November 20, 1765.

The famous "Bolero" of Ravel was dedicated to Ida Rubinstein and first produced by her as a ballet in Paris on November 20, 1928.

Daniel Gregory Mason was born November 20, 1873.

November Twenty-first

  Simplicity, truth and naturalness are the great principles of the beautiful in all productions of art. --Gluck

Henry Purcell died November 21, 1695.

Leopold Godowsky died November 21, 1938.

Artur Rubinstein made an historical appearance in America as soloist of the New York Philharmonic on November 21, 1937.

Eugene Istomin made his debut with the New York Philharmonic on November 21, 1943.

World premiere of Meyerbeer's "Robert Le Diable" took place in Paris November 21, 1831.

November Twenty-second
  (Day of St. Cecilia, patron saint of music)

    St. Cecilia's Day
  In a consort of voices,
    while instruments play,

> With music we celebrate
>   this holy day.
> To Cecilia. --
>
>   Christopher Fishburn

St. Cecilia, patron saint of music.

On the 22nd of November, 1683, a group of musicians started a "Musical Society" in London to celebrate the "Festival of St. Cecilia, a great patroness of music."

Benjamin Britten was born November 22, 1913.

Gunther Schuller was born November 22, 1925.

Christine Nilsson died November 22, 1921.

Elisabeth Rethburg made her Metropolitan debut on November 22, 1922, as Aida.

Arthur S. Sullivan died November 22, 1900.

November Twenty-third

> His (Wagner) opera is like a string of beads, each bead
> being a glittering and intoxicating tune. --Danreuther

On November 23, 1885, the occasion being Anton Seidl's debut as a conductor in the United States, "Lohengrin" was
given as the opening opera of the season.   Seidl's wife,
Auguste Seidl-Kraus, was the Elso while the Ortrud was
Marianne Brandt.

Manuel de Falla was born November 23, 1877.

Metropolitan premiere of "Il Barbiere di Siviglia" was presented on November 23, 1883, with Marcella Sembrich as
Rosina.   Augusto Vianesi conducted.

Berlioz' "Harold in Italy" was first performed November 23,
1834, at the Paris Conservatoire with the composer conducting.

Arthur Bodansky died November 23, 1939.

Johann Bottlob Breitkopf was born November 23, 1719.

Raymond Lewanthal made his New York debut November 23,
1965, at Town Hall.

November Twenty-fourth

> Without enthusiasm one will never accomplish anything
> in art. --Schumann

Adelina Patti made her operatic debut on November 24, 1859,
in New York, singing Lucia.   She was sixteen years old.

Enrico Caruso made his New York debut November 24, 1903,
appearing in "Rigoletto."

Metropolitan debut of Jussi Bjoerling occurred on November
24, 1938.

Lilli Lehmann was born November 24, 1848.

Henriette Voight was born November 24, 1803.

November Twenty-fifth

> ....words seem to me so ambiguous, so vague, so
> easily misunderstandable in comparison with genuine
> music, which fills the soul with things a thousand times
> better than words.--Mendelssohn

Yehudi Menuhin made his historic New York appearance, at
the age of eleven, when he played the Beethoven Concerto
with the New York Symphony Society on November 25, 1927.
Fritz Busch conducted.

William Kempff was born November 25, 1895.

Virgil Thomson was born November 25, 1896.

American debut of Giuseppe de Luca was presented on November 25, 1915, at the Metropolitan Opera.

"Martha" by Von Flotow was first performed November 25,
1847, in Vienna. Leading roles at the world premiere were
sung by Anna Zerr and Karl Formes.

Helen Jepson was born November 25, 1906.

Ethelbert Nevin was born November 25, 1862.

Metropolitan premiere of "Hansel und Gretel" was given on
November 25, 1905, under the direction of Alfred Hertz.

November Twenty-sixth

> A work of art is a corner of creation seen through a
> temperament.--Zola

The triumphal Metropolitan debut of Joan Sutherland took
place on November 26, 1961, as Lucia.

Geraldine Farrar's American debut was on November 26,
1906, at the Metropolitan Opera in "Romeo et Juliette."

Eugene Istomin was born November 26, 1925.

November Twenty-seventh

> Every person has a lead with which he attempts to meas-
> ure the depth of art. The string of some is long, that
> of others is very short; yet each thinks he has reached
> the bottom, while in reality art is a bottomless deep
> that none have as yet fully explored, and probably none
> ever will. Art is endless!--Schopenhauer

The first performance of Handel's "Dettingen te Deum" was
on November 27, 1743.

Sir Julius Benedict was born November 27, 1804.

Guillaume Dufay, the first genius of the early Flemish Renaissance, died November 27, 1474.

American debut of Ania Dorfmann occurred November 27,
1936, in Town Hall, New York.

Metropolitan premiere of Wagner's "Der Fliegende Hollander"
was presented on November 27, 1889.

Ludwig Rellstab died November 27, 1860.

Balfe's "Bohemian Girl" was first produced on November 27,
1843, in London.

Metropolitan debut of Mario Del Monaco was on November
27, 1950, in Puccini's "Manon Lescaut."

The Teatro Costanzi in Rome was opened November 27, 1880,
with "Semiramide."

November Twenty-eighth

> With Ferdinand Ries I pass very musical hours. Kindred
> sympathies are fostered and a lasting friendship pro-
> moted by a profound veneration for Beethoven, the master
> of Ries.--Moschele's diary

Ferdinand Ries was born November 28, 1784.

First public performance of Beethoven's last piano concerto
No. 5, the "Emperor," took place in the Gewandhaus, Leipzig on November 28, 1811, with Friedrich Schneider as

soloist.

Anton Rubinstein was born November 28, 1829.

Metropolitan premiere of "Guillaume Tell" was presented on November 28, 1884, under the baton of Leopold Damrosch.

Rose Bampton was born November 28, 1909.

Metropolitan debut of Rose Bampton took place November 28, 1932, on her twenty-third birthday.

Jose Iturbi was born November 28, 1895.

American debut of Louis Kentner took place in Town Hall, New York, on November 28, 1956.

Rosa Raisa made her American debut on November 28, 1913, as Aida.

November Twenty-ninth

> He (Donizetti) is remarkable as an instance of freshness of fancy brought on by incessant manufacture. Such a change is almost exclusively confined to Italian genius in its workings. It learns and grows while creating.--
> Chorley

Gaetano Donizetti was born November 29, 1797.

Giacomo Puccini died November 29, 1924.

Giulia Grisi died November 29, 1869.

Joseph Krips' first performance as conductor and musical director of the San Francisco Symphony took place on November 29, 1963.

American debut of prodigy Josef Hofmann was on November 29, 1887, in a concert at the Metropolitan Opera House. The child astonished the audience--he was a marvel!

Benno Moiseiwitsch made his American debut at Carnegie Hall, New York, on November 29, 1919.

Ettore Panizza died November 29, 1967.

Giacomo Puccini,
died November 29, 1924.

Metropolitan debut of Emma Calvé was given on November 29, 1893, in "Cavalleria Rusticana."

Claudio Monteverdi died November 29, 1643.

Metropolitan debut of John McCormack occurred November 29, 1910, in "La Traviata."

Jan Peerce made his Metropolitan debut as Alfredo in "La Traviata" on November 29, 1941.

Nellie Melba sang a last Violetta in "La Traviata" on November 29, 1910, at the Metropolitan.

Pol Plancon sang Mefistofeles for his American debut on November 29, 1893, at the Metropolitan Opera.

American debut of Nathan Milstein took place on November 29, 1929, with the St. Louis Symphony.

Metropolitan premiere of "Don Giovanni" was heard on November 29, 1883, with Christine Nilsson, Marcella Sembrich and Italo Campanini in the cast.

Harold Schonberg was born November 29, 1915.

Jean Baptiste Lully was born November 29, 1632.

Sofia Scalchi was born November 29, 1850.

November Thirtieth

> Every artist of genius breathes into his work an unex-
> pressed idea, which speaks to our feelings even before
> it can be defined. --Franz Liszt

Beniamino Gigli, greatest of the post-Caruso tenors, died
November 30, 1957.

Caffarelli died November 30, 1783.

Eleanor Spencer, pianist and first president of The Leschetizky Association, was born on November 30, 1890.

Wilhelm Furtwaengler died November 30, 1954.

Ernest Newman, English music critic, was born November
30, 1868.

Ludwig Thuille was born November 30, 1861.

DECEMBER

Exalt art, and art will elevate you. --<u>Booth</u>

December First

Contact with the powers of others calls forth new ones in ourselves. --<u>Von Weber</u>

American premiere of Wagner's "Tristan und Isolde" took place December 1, 1886. It was a sensation and became a favorite in New York. Anton Seidl conducted the premiere.

Franz Liszt made his first appearance as pianist on December 1, 1822. He was eleven years old.

Metropolitan debut of Dorothy Kirsten as Mimi in "La Boheme" was presented on December 1, 1945.

Hoffmeister and Kuhnel organized a music publishing firm on December 1, 1800, which later became C. F. Peters, Leipzig.

Metropolitan debut of Richard Bonelli as Germont in "La Traviata" took place on December 1, 1932.

World premiere of Britten's "Billy Budd" was given December 1, 1951, at Covent Garden, London, with the composer conducting.

December Second

He (Brahms) has burst upon us fully equipped, as Minerva sprang from the head of Jupiter. --<u>Schumann</u>

The Third Symphony of Johannes Brahms was heard for the first time December 2, 1883, in Vienna.

Joseph Lhevinne died December 2, 1944.

Dinu Lipatti died December 2, 1950.

"Samson and Delilah" (Saint-Saens) was first performed December 2, 1877, in Weimar.

Vincent D'Indy died December 2, 1931.

The premiere of Donizetti's "La Favorite" was on December 2, 1840, in Paris. Rosine Stoltz created the role of Leonora di Guzman.

Sir John Barbirolli was born December 2, 1899.

Dinu Lipatti died December 2, 1950.

Sir Paola Tosti died December 2, 1916.

December Third

   At every step Fame gathers strength. --Virgil

Maria Callas was born December 3, 1923.

Giovanni Martinelli made his concert debut on December 3, 1910, in Milan.

Gershwin's "Rhapsody in Blue" was first performed December 3, 1925, in New York.

Metropolitan premiere of "Elektra" took place December 3, 1932, under the direction of Artur Bodanzky.

Anton Von Webern was born December 3, 1883.

Elgar's First Symphony was heard for the first time December 3, 1908, in Manchester.

Christian Sinding died December 3, 1941.

December Fourth

   What love is to the heart, music is to the other arts
   and to man, for music is love itself. --Weber

Schumann's Piano Concerto in A minor was introduced December 4, 1845, in Dresden, with Clara Schumann playing the solo part.

Nellie Melba's debut as Lucia was on December 4, 1893.

Tchaikowsky's Violin Concerto in D Major was first performed December 4, 1881, in Vienna.   Adolf Brodsky was
soloist.

Patrice Munsell made her bow at the Metropolitan on December 4, 1943, in "Mignon."

The debut of Claudia Muzio as Tosca was on December 4,
1916, at the Metropolitan Opera with Caruso and Scotti.

Daniel Gregory Mason died December 4, 1953.

December Fifth

> O Mozart! If I could instill into the soul of every lover
> of music the admiration I have for his matchless works,
> all countries would seek to be possessed of so great a
> treasure. --Haydn

Wolfgang Amadeus Mozart died December 5, 1791.

World premiere of the "Symphonie Fantastique" by Berlioz
was given December 5, 1830, in Paris.   The concert was a
great success.

The American Opera Society presented Joan Sutherland in a
concert performance of "La Sonnambula" at Carnegie Hall on
December 5, 1961.

Jeanette Scovotti was born December 5, 1933.

Metropolitan premiere of "Lucrezia Borgia" took place December 5, 1904, with Enrico Caruso, Edyth Walker and Antonio Scotti in the cast.   Arturo Vigna conducted.

Hans Richter died December 5, 1916.

The first Metropolitan performance of "Mefistofele" was
given on December 5, 1883, with Christine Nilsson, Zelia
Trebelli and Italo Campanini.

Metropolitan premiere performance of "Fedora" was presented
on December 5, 1906, with Lina Cavalieri, Enrico Caruso
and Antonio Scotti.

Grace Moore was born December 5, 1901.

December Sixth

> The key to the understanding of contemporary music lies
> in repeated hearing; one must hear it till it sounds fam-
> iliar, until one begins to notice false notes if they are
> played. --Sessions

Jan Kubelik died December 6, 1940.

Metropolitan debut of Regina Resnik as Lenora in "Il Trovatore" took place December 6, 1944.

Luigi Lablache was born December 6, 1794.

Wilhelmine Schroeder-Devrient was born December 6, 1804.

Astrid Varnay made her debut at the Metropolitan on December 6, 1941, as Sieglinde in "Die Walkure."

"Les Troyen" by Berlioz was first performed in German on
December 6, 1890.

Barbara Marchisio was born December 6, 1833.

Louis Gilbert Duprez was born December 6, 1806.

December Seventh

> If all were determined to play the first violin we should
> never have a complete orchestra.   Therefore respect
> every musician in his proper place. --Schumann

The first concert given by the Philharmonic Society of New
York (New York Philharmonic) was on December 7, 1842.

La Scala debut of Maria Callas occurred on December 7,
1951, in the role of Elena in Verdi's "I Vespri Siciliani."

Pietro Mascagni was born December 7, 1863.

Frances Alda made her Metropolitan debut as Gilda in "Rigoletto" December 7, 1908.

Ernst Toch was born December 7, 1887.

Carl Fischer was born December 7, 1849.

Rudolf Friml was born December 7, 1879.

Eleanor Steber made her bow at the Metropolitan Opera on December 7, 1940.

Kirsten Flagstad died December 7, 1962.

Clara Haskil died December 7, 1960.

December Eighth

> Art! Who can say that he fathoms it? Who is there capable of discussing the nature of this great goddess?-- Beethoven

World premiere of Beethoven's Seventh Symphony was presented on December 8, 1813, in the large hall of the University of Vienna with Beethoven conducting.

Jean Sibelius was born December 8, 1865.

Maestro Tullio Serafin was born December 8, 1878.

Paris heard Rossini's "Semiramide" for the first time on December 8, 1825, at the Theatre-Italien.

World premiere of Verdi's "Luisa Miller" was presented at the Teatro San Carlo in Naples on December 8, 1849.

Xaver Scharwenka died December 8, 1924.

Alexander Siloti died December 8, 1945.

Wieland Wagner's new production of "Lohengrin" was unveiled at the Metropolitan Opera on December 8, 1966.

Bohuslav Martinu was born December 8, 1890.

Ernest Schelling died December 8, 1940.

Carlotta Marchisio was born December 8, 1835.

December Ninth

> The artist can show his or her skill in simple things, as well as in great. If the great works are as the mighty ocean, those little gems are as the pearls found beneath the waters.--Merz

December

Elisabeth Schwarzkopf was born December 9, 1915.

American premiere of "Der Rosenkavalier" was given on December 9, 1913, at the Metropolitan Opera with Alfred Hertz conducting.

Metropolitan debut of George Szell took place on December 9, 1942, with "Salome."

The world premiere performance of "Salome" was produced on December 9, 1905, at the Royal Opera in Dresden. Ernst von Schuch conducted.

Franz Kullak died December 9, 1913.

December Tenth

> Faith in his subject is an indispensable requisite in the work of an artist. --Mendelssohn

Cesar Franck was born December 10, 1822.

Mischa Elman made his American debut in New York on December 10, 1908, performing the Tchaikowsky Violin Concerto with the Russian Symphony Orchestra.

World premiere of "La Fanciulla del West" was on December 10, 1910, at the Metropolitan Opera in New York. Arturo Toscanini conducted and the cast included Emmy Destinn, Enrico Caruso and Antonio Scotti.

Morton Gould was born December 10, 1913.

December Eleventh

> The worth of art appears most eminent in music, since it requires no material, no subject-matter, whose effect must be deducted; it is wholly form and power, and it raises and ennobles whatever it expresses. --Goethe

Hector Berlioz was born December 11, 1803.

Metropolitan debut of Jess Thomas took place on December 11, 1962, as Walter in "Die Meistersinger."

Hector Berlioz,
born December 11, 1803.

Giovanni Matteo Mario died December 11, 1883.

"I Pagliacci" had its American premiere at the Metropolitan Opera with Nellie Melba and Mario Ancona on December 11, 1893.

Elliott Carter was born December 11, 1908.

Leo Ornstein was born December 11, 1895.

Giocomo Lauri-Volpi was born December 11, 1892.

December Twelfth

    Yea, music is the Prophet's art
    Among the gifts that God hath sent,
    One of the most magnificent!--

                    Longfellow

Kirsten Flagstad made her operatic debut on December 12,

1913.

Kurt Atterberg was born December 12, 1887.

Francisco Curt Lange was born December 12, 1903.

Albert Carre died December 12, 1938.

December Thirteenth

> Music is love; it springs from religion and leads to
> religion. --Hanslick

Pauline Anna Milder-Hauptmann was born December 13, 1785.
Beethoven wrote the part of Leonora (Fidelio) for her.

John Charles Thomas died December 13, 1960.

Josef Lhevinne was born December 13, 1874.

Stravinsky's "Symphonie des Psaumes" was first performed
on December 13, 1930, in Brussels.

Marisa Morel was born December 13, 1914.

December Fourteenth

> It hath been anciently held and observed that the sense
> of hearing and the kind of music have most operation
> upon manners. --Bacon

Rosalyn Tureck was born December 14, 1914.

Tobias Matthay died December 14, 1945.

Carl Philipp Emanuel Bach died December 14, 1788.

Metropolitan premiere of "Romeo et Juliette" took place on
December 14, 1891, with Emma Eames and Jean and Edouard
de Reszke.

The first performance of "Gianni Schicchi" was on December
14, 1918, at the Metropolitan Opera in New York. The cast
included Florence Easton, Giuseppe de Luca and Adamo
Didur.

World premiere of "Wozzeck" took place December 14, 1925, at the Berlin Staatsoper under the direction of Erich Kleiber.

Luigi Marchesi died December 14, 1829.

December Fifteenth

> Goethe's poems have great power over me, not only be-cause of their contents but because of their rhythm. I am attuned and stimulated to composition by his language which builds itself to lofty heights as if by the work of spirits and already bears within itself the mystery of the harmonies. --Beethoven

Dvorak's "New World Symphony" was introduced by the New York Philharmonic Orchestra under Anton Seidl on December 15, 1893.

Robert Merrill made his debut at the Metropolitan on Decem-ber 15, 1945, as Germont père in "La Traviata."

December Sixteenth

> Music is the mediator between the spiritual and sensual life. Although the spirit be not master of that which it creates through music, yet it is blessed in this recrea-tion, which, like every creation of art, is mightier than the artist. --Beethoven

Ludwig van Beethoven was born December 16, 1770.

Camille Saint-Saens died December 16, 1921.

The Third Symphony of Bruckner was dedicated to Bruckner's idol, Richard Wagner, and was first performed December 16, 1877, in Vienna.

Zoltan Kodaly was born December 16, 1882.

Arthur Bodansky was born December 16, 1877.

James McCracken was born December 16, 1926.

Ludwig van Beethoven,
born December 16, 1770.

December Seventeenth

Schubert was like a gardener bewildered with the luxuri-
ant growth springing up around him. As fast as his
ideas arose they were poured forth on paper. He was
too rich for himself--his fancy outgrew his powers of
arrangement.--Haweis

The "Unfinished" Symphony in B Minor of Franz Schubert
was first performed in Vienna on December 17, 1865. Schubert never heard the symphony.

Rise Stevens' Metropolitan debut as "Mignon" took place on

December 17, 1938, with Richard Crooks and Ezio Pinza.

Arthur Fiedler was born December 17, 1894.

Peter Warlock died December 17, 1930.

Zinka Milanov made her American debut at the Metropolitan Opera on December 17, 1937, in "Il Trovatore."

December Eighteenth

> There is something marvelous in music. I might almost say it is, in itself, a marvel. Its position is somewhere between the region of thought and that of phenomena; a glimmering medium between mind and matter, related to both and yet differing from either. Spiritual, and yet requiring rhythm; material, and yet independent of space. --H. Heine

Birgit Nilsson gave a sensational Metropolitan debut on December 18, 1959, as Isolde.

Antonio Stradivari died December 18, 1737.

Camille Pleyel was born December 18, 1788.

Moriz Rosenthal was born December 18, 1862.

Bruckner's Eighth Symphony was first played on December 18, 1892, in Vienna with Hans Richter conducting.

Louis Moreau Gottschalk died December 18, 1869.

Edward MacDowell was born December 18, 1861.

December Nineteenth

> A distinguished philosopher spoke of architecture as frozen music, and his assertion caused many to shake their heads. We believe this really beautiful idea could not be better reintroduced than by calling architecture silent music. --Goethe

Cleofonte Campanini died December 19, 1919.

Fritz Reiner was born December 19, 1888.

Desmond Dupre was born December 19, 1916.

Metropolitan debut of John Alexander occurred on December 19, 1961.

Milka Ternina was born December 19, 1863.

Dusolina Giannini was born December 19, 1902.

December Twentieth

The secret of life is in art. --Oscar Wilde

Emma Calvé as Carmen.

The New York premiere of "Carmen" was on December 20, 1893, when Emma Calvé made her memorable debut.

"Semiramide" was produced in New York on December 20, 1882, with Adelina Patti and Sofia Scalchi.

Henry Hadley was born December 20, 1871.

Metropolitan premiere of "La Gioconda" was presented on December 20, 1883, with Christine Nilsson, Sofia Scalchi and Giuseppe del Puente.

December Twenty-first

> Music must take rank as the highest of the fine arts--
> as the one which, more than any other, ministers to
> human welfare.--Herbert Spencer

Metropolitan premiere of "Luisa Miller" was on December 21, 1929.   Tullio Serafin was the conductor and the cast included Rosa Ponselle, Marion Telva, Giacomo Lauri-Volpi and Giuseppe de Luca.

Ernst Pauer was born December 21, 1826.

On December 21, 1932, the Ponselle sisters appeared in the same Metropolitan performance of "La Gioconda."

Niels Gade died December 21, 1890.

Charles Lamoureux died December 21, 1899.

December Twenty-second

> To describe a scene is the province of the painter.   The
> poet, too, has the advantage over me, for his range is
> less limited than mine.   On the other hand, my sphere
> extends to regions which to them are not easily accessi-
> ble.--Beethoven

The first performance of Beethoven's Pastoral Symphony and his Fifth Symphony took place in Vienna at the Theater-an-der-Wien, December 22, 1808.

Theresa Carreño was born December 22, 1853.

Edouard de Reszke was born December 22, 1853.

Louise Homer made her operatic debut in "Aida" on December 22, 1900, in San Francisco.

Theresa Carreño,
born December 22, 1853.

DeBussy's exquisite orchestral prelude, "L'Apres-midi d'un faune," was first introduced at a concert in Paris on December 22, 1894.

Edgar Varese was born December 22, 1885.

Andre Kostelanetz was born December 22, 1901.

Deems Taylor was born December 22, 1885.

Metropolitan debut of Maestro Ettore Panizza took place on December 22, 1934, when he directed "Aida."

Leopoldo Mugnone died December 22, 1941.

Walter Damrosch died December 22, 1950.

December Twenty-third

>   What shines and glitters has its birth
>   But for the present hour alone;
>   The Real--the thing of truth and worth--
>   To all posterity goes down.--
>
>   Goethe

Giacomo Puccini was born December 23, 1858.

Beethoven composed his Violin Concerto in D Major for Franz Clement who introduced the masterpiece on December 23, 1806, at the Theater-an-der Wien.

American debut of Enrico Caruso took place on December 23, 1903, in "Rigoletto" with Marcella Sembrich as Gilda.

Metropolitan premiere of "Don Carlos" was presented on December 23, 1920, with Rosa Ponselle, Giovanni Martinelli, Giuseppe De Luca and Adamo Didur. The conductor was Gennaro Papi.

"Hansel and Gretel" (Humperdinck) was heard for the first time on December 23, 1893, at the Hoftheater in Weimar.

Anton Seidl conducted the first Metropolitan performance of "Euryanthe" on December 23, 1887. The cast included Lilli Lehmann, Marianne Brandt, Max Alvary and Emil Fischer.

December Twenty-fourth

> The most despairing songs are the most beautiful, and I know some immortal ones that are pure tears. --
> Alfred De Musset

Enrico Caruso gave his last performance on December 24, 1920, in "La Juive" at the Metropolitan Opera in New York. It was his farewell to the Metropolitan and to opera.

Lucrezia Bori was born December 24, 1887.

Alban Berg died December 24, 1935.

John Dunstable died December 24, 1453.

Adamo Didur was born December 24, 1874.

World premiere performance of Verdi's "Aida" was presented in Cairo, Egypt, on December 24, 1871. The conductor for the premiere was Giovanni Bottesini.

Metropolitan premiere of "Parsifal" took place on December 24, 1903, under the direction of Alfred Hertz.

December Twenty-fifth

> Let nothing you dismay,
> For Jesus Christ, our Savior,
> Was born upon this day. --
> <u>Anonymous old carol</u>

The first performance of J. S. Bach's Christmas Oratorio was given on December 25, 1734, in Leipzig.

"Dido and Aeneas" was first performed on Christmas Day in 1689, in London.

J. A. Hiller was born December 25, 1728.

Gladys Swarthout was born Christmas Day in 1904.

The first concert by the Handel and Haydn Society, Boston, was given December 25, 1815.

Liszt's daughter, Cosima, was born December 25, 1837.

Raoul Gunsbourg was born December 25, 1859.

December Twenty-sixth

> Music requires inspiration. --<u>Gluck</u>

The first performance of Gluck's opera, "Alceste," was given on December 26, 1767, at the Burgtheater in Vienna. The Alceste of the original production was Antonia Bernasconi.

World premiere of Donizetti's "Anna Bolena" took place at the Teatro Carcano in Milan on December 26, 1830. The original cast included Giuditta Pasta and Giovanni-Battista Rubini.

Bellini's "Norma" was heard for the first time on December 26, 1831, at La Scala, opening the Carnival season in Milan, with Giuditta Pasta as the tragic priestess Norma.

World premiere of "Lucrezia Borgia" by Donizetti was presented at La Scala on December 26, 1833. The Lucrezia Borgia of the original production was Henriette-Clementine Meric-Lalande.

The world premiere of "Sadko" by Rimsky-Korsakov was

given in Moscow December 26, 1897.

Metropolitan premiere of Puccini's "La Boheme" took place December 26, 1900, with Nellie Melba as Mimi.

December Twenty-seventh

> I am sure if anything on earth can give an idea of the angelic choir, it must be the music of Palestrina!--
> Baroness Bunsen

Giovanni Pierluigi da Palestrina was born December 27, 1525.

The music of Palestrina--
"an idea of the angelic choir."

The debut of Antonio Scotti in "Don Giovanni" took place on December 27, 1899.

Frieda Hempel made her American debut December 27, 1912, at the Metropolitan in New York.

Willem van Otterloo was born December 27, 1907.

Charles Munch made his American debut on December 27, 1946, with the Boston Symphony Orchestra.

Oscar Levant was born December 27, 1906.

December Twenty-eighth

> As the study of geometry trains the mind in the abstract, so the study of music trains the emotions in the abstract. --Anon.

Maurice Ravel died December 28, 1937.

Metropolitan debut of Luisa Tetrazzini as Lucia took place on December 28, 1911.

Francesco Tamagno was born December 28, 1850.

American premiere of Weber's "Oberon" was given on December 28, 1918, at the Metropolitan Opera with Rosa Ponselle and Giovanni Martinelli.

Helen Traubel made her bow at the Metropolitan on December 28, 1939.

Roger Sessions was born December 28, 1896.

Stravinsky conducted a performance of his opera "Le Roussignol" in Washington, D.C., on December 28, 1960. Reri Grist was the highly praised Nightingale.

December Twenty-ninth

> The greatest respect an artist can pay to music is to give it life. --Pablo Casals

Pablo Casals was born December 29, 1876.

Giuseppe de Luca was born December 29, 1876.

The first concert by the San Francisco Symphony Orchestra was given on December 29, 1911.

Momentous debut of Zubin Mehta at the Metropolitan Opera, in Verdi's "Aida," took place on December 29, 1965.

December Thirtieth

> In Mendelssohn we admire most his great talent for form; his power of appropriating all that is most piquant, his charmingly beautiful workmanship, his delicate sensitiveness and his earnest, I might almost say his impassioned, equanimity.--Heinrich Heine

The De Reszke's made their debut in "Siegfried" on December 30, 1877.

Andre Messager was born December 30, 1853.

Bruckner's most popular Symphony, the Seventh in E Major, dedicated to King Ludwig II of Bavaria, was first performed under the baton of Arthur Nikisch in Leipzig on December 30, 1884.

World premiere performance of Brahms' Second Symphony was given on December 30, 1877, with Hans Richter conducting.

Dimitri Kabalevsky was born December 30, 1904.

The Metropolitan premiere of "Cavalleria Rusticana" was presented on December 30, 1891. Augusto Vianesi conducted.

"Prince Igor" was first heard at the Metropolitan on December 30, 1915. The chief singers were Adamo Didur, Pasquale Amato and Frances Alda.

Paul Wranitzky was born December 30, 1756.

December Thirty-first

> An enemy is always a keen searcher for faults, while a friend seeks to find also our good qualifications. The critic should be a friend.--Merz

Nathan Milstein was born December 31, 1904.

Alexander Lambert died December 31, 1929.

Index of Names

Absil, Jean (composer), 162
Academie des Operas, 48
Academy of Music, New York, 152
Adler, Kurt (conductor and manager), 65
Albanese, Licia (soprano), 121
Albeniz, Isaac (pianist and composer), 89, 96
Albinoni, Tomasco (composer and violinist), 101
Alboni, Marietta (contralto), 50, 108
Alda, Frances (soprano), 73, 97, 145, 191
Alexander, John (tenor), 199
Alvary, Max (tenor), 81, 171
Amati, Niccolo (violin-maker), 130, 139
Ambros, August Wilhelm (composer and pianist), 177
American Conservatory of Music, 108
American Guild of Organists, 72
American Music Center, 36
American Musicological Society, 99
American Opera Society, 190
Amon, Johann Andreas (horn virtuoso), 63
Amram, David (composer), 177
Ancona, Mario (baritone), 41, 45
Anderson, Marion (contralto), 10, 37, 137
Anrooy, Peter van (conductor and composer), 157
Antonini, Alfredo (conductor), 97
Arditi, Luigi (composer and conductor), 121
Arensky, Anton (composer), 43, 130
Arne, Thomas (composer), 49, 54, 126
Arrau, Claudio (pianist), 29, 30
Ansermet, Ernest (conductor), 40, 173
Arbatsky, Yury (composer and musicologist), 73
Ashkenazy, Vladimir (pianist), 114
Atterberg, Kurt (conductor and composer), 195
Auer, Leopold (violinist and teacher), 101, 118
Austin, Frederic (baritone and composer), 63

Baccaloni, Salvatore (bass), 72
Bach, Carl Philipp Emanuel (harpsichordist and composer),
    51, 195
Bach Gesellschaft, 124

Bach, Johann Christian (pianist and composer), 7, 141
Bach, Johann Sebastian (composer and organist), 58, 123, 131
    "Passion According to St. John, " 61
    "Passion According to St. Matthew, " 53, 59
    "Christmas Oratorio, " 203
Bach Society, 116
Bach, Wilhelm Friedemann (organist and composer), 112
Bachauer, Gina (pianist), 91, 165
Backhaus, Wilhelm (Pianist), 61
Baduro-Skoda, Paul (pianist), 153
Baillot, Pierre Marie (violinist), 144, 151
Balakirev, Mily (composer), 8, 96
Balfe, Michael William (composer), 88, 160
    "Bohemian Girl, " 184
Bampton, Rose (soprano), 185
Banti, Brigitta (soprano), 39
Bantock, Sir Granville (composer and conductor), 128, 158
Barber, Samuel (composer), 52
    "Vanessa, " 15
Barbieri, Fedora (mezzo-soprano), 99
Barbirolli, Sir John (conductor), 189
Barere, Simon (pianist), 65, 139
Bartok, Bela (composer), 61, 148
Bastianini, Ettore (baritone), 21, 148
Bauer, Harold (pianist), 54, 78
Baum, Kurt (tenor), 55
Bax, Sir Arnold (composer), 152, 171
Bayreuth Festspielhaus, 91, 131
Beale, William (organist and composer), 81
Bechstein, Friedrich (piano maker), 50, 98
Beck, Sydney, 139
Beecham, Sir Thomas (conductor), 13, 51, 78, 168, 173
Beethoven, Ludwig van (composer), 61, 63, 83, 196
    "Symphony No. 1, " 65
    "Symphony No. 2, " 73
    "Symphony No. 3, " (Eroica), 68
    "Symphony No. 4, " 175
    "Symphony No. 5, " 200
    "Symphony No. 6, " (Pastoral), 200
    "Symphony No. 7, " 192
    "Symphony No. 8, " 44
    "Symphony No. 9, " 83
    "Fidelio, " 91, 178, 179
    "Missa Solemnis, " 68, 111
    "Overture to Egmont, " 92
    "Piano Concerto No. 3, " 67
    "Piano Concerto No. 5, " 184

Beethoven, Ludwig van (cont.)
  "Violin Concerto in D Major," 202
Beinum, Eduard van (conductor), 72, 140
Bellezza, Vincenzo (conductor), 31, 38
Bellini, Vincenzo (composer), 147, 152, 168
  "Beatrice di Tenda," 55
  "Capuleti, I, ed I Montecchi," 53
  "Norma," 203
  "Il Pirata," 164
  "I Puritani," 20
  "La Sonnambula," 50, 124, 175
  "La Staniera," 35
Benda, Georg (composer and pianist), 111
Benedict, Sir Julius (composer and conductor), 100, 184
Benjamin, Arthur (composer), 145
Bennett, Robert Russell (composer), 105
Berg, Alban (composer), 32, 202
  "Lulu," 99
  "Wozzeck," 57, 196
Berganza, Teresa (mezzo-soprano), 56
Bergen Symphony Orchestra, 154
Bergonzi, Carlo (tenor), 118, 174
Berkshire Music Center, 115
Berkshire Symphonic Festival, 134
Berlioz, Hector (composer), 51, 193
  "Beatrice et Benedict," 129
  "Benvenuto Cellini," 143
  "La Damnation de Faust," 38
  "Les Troyen," 191
  "Harold in Italy," 182
  "Symphonie Fantastique," 190
Bernacchi, Antonio (male soprano), 108
Bernstein, Leonard (conductor and composer), 89, 136, 174
  "Jeremiah," 24
Bertini, Henry (pianist), 151, 164
Biancolli, Louis (music critic), 74
Biber, Franz von (violinist and composer), 81, 130
Biggs, E. Power (organist), 63
Billington, Elizabeth (soprano), 136
Bing, Rudolf (opera impresario), 12
Bizet, Georges (composer), 99, 163
  "Carmen," 48, 199
Bjorling, Jussi (tenor), 9, 28, 142, 182
Blacher, Boris (composer), 8
  "Fluchtversuch," 28
Bliss, Arthur (composer), 126
Blitzstein, Marc (pianist and composer), 47
Bloch, Ernest (composer), 199, 122

Gedda, Nicolai (tenor), 117
Gehrkens, Karl W. (musical editor and educator), 74
Gershwin, George (composer), 116, 148
    "Porgy and Bess, " 150
    "Rhapsody in Blue, " 34, 189
Geza, Anda (pianist), 178
Giannini, Dusolina (soprano), 199
Gibbons, Orlando (composer), 100
Gieseking, Walter (pianist and composer), 12, 163, 169
Gigli, Beniamino (tenor), 57, 95, 179, 187
Gilels, Emil (pianist), 160
Giordano, Umberto (composer), 136, 173
    "Andrea Chenier, " 51, 62
    "Fedora, " 177, 190
Giulini, Carla Maria (conductor), 84
Glazunov, Alexander (composer), 59, 129
Gliere, Reinhold (composer), 13
    "The Red Poppy, " 104
Glinka, Michael (composer), 36, 98
Gluck, Christoph Willibald von (composer), 112, 175
    "Alceste, " 203
    "Armide, " 147, 175
    "Iphigenie en Aulide, " 74
    "Iphigenie en Tauride, " 90
    "Orpheo ed Eurydice, " 153
Gobbi, Tito (baritone), 162
Godard, Benjamin (composer), 12, 133
Goddard, Arabella (pianist), 13, 68
Godowsky, Leopold (pianist and composer), 34, 180
Goehr, Walter (composer and conductor), 67
Goetschius, Percy (Professor of Music), 138
Goldmark, Karl (composer and teacher), 8, 90
Goldmark, Rubin (composer and teacher), 50, 131
Goldovsky, Boris (opera producer and conductor), 101
Goldsand, Robert (pianist), 56, 59
Goldschmidt, Berthold (composer and conductor), 17
Goodson, Katherine (pianist), 16, 17, 106
Goosens, Eugene (conductor and composer), 93, 104, 108
Gorodnitzki, Sasha (pianist), 92
Gottschalk, Louis M. (pianist and composer), 84, 198
Gould, Glen (pianist), 7, 48, 148
Gould, Morton (pianist and composer), 193
Gounod, Charles (composer), 105, 159
    "Faust, " 57
    "Romeo and Juliet, " 77, 195
Graf, Herbert (opera producer), 70
Graffman, Gary (pianist), 157
Grainger, Percy (pianist and composer), 33, 115